Play With Me Fuse

Mhairi O'Reilly

Copyright © 2024 Mhairi O'Reilly

Kindle Edition
Paperback
Hardcover

Written by Mhairi O'Reilly
All rights reserved. No part of this publication may be
reproduced, distributed or transmitted in any form or
by any
means, or stored in a database or retrieval system,
without the
prior written permission of the publisher.

Disclaimer: The material in this book is for mature
audiences
only and contains graphic content. It is intended only
for
those aged 18 and older.

This book is a work of fiction. Any names, places,
characters,
or incidents are a figment of the author's imagination.
Any
resemblance to persons living or dead or actual
events is
purely coincidental

Dream On, Dream On,
Dream On Dream until your dreams come true.
 -Aerosmith

1

I walked into the room, the last to take a seat for Church. The heavy scrape of my chair echoed in the silence as all eyes turned to me. The weight of their stares was clear: disapproval. Yeah, they could fuck off.

Sure, I was hungover, and yeah, I looked like shit. Big deal.

"Nice of you to join us, Fuse," Shadow said, his smirk cutting through the haze in my pounding head. He leaned back in his chair, arms crossed like he owned the world—which, to be fair, he kind of did in my book.

I swallowed the retort bubbling up in my throat. My head hurt too much to bother arguing the fact that I wasn't late—I'd walked in right on time. Shadow had been on my case lately, though, as had a few others. They thought I was partying too hard. Maybe they were right. The booze and women had become my escape hatch in the past few months, filling a void I couldn't name. Not that I'd admit that to anyone.

Shadow's voice pulled me from my thoughts. "Let's get started. Black and West are back from Philadelphia. Cross is leading the Fire Dragons now. If you remember, he's the son of the former President—batshit crazy and twice as dangerous. The club is in chaos. Members are dropping like flies because they don't want to follow him. He's leading them straight off a cliff."

The name Cross sent a ripple of unease through the room. Even hungover, I could feel it.

"What's the money situation with them?" I asked, regretting it instantly as the words sent a fresh stab of pain through my skull. "I'm sure we're not the only club they've stolen from."

Kickstand, always glued to his laptop, spoke up. "That's been harder to track. Cross is paranoid as hell. Sources say he's keeping the money close—won't even let his officers in on the finances."

Black added, his voice a deep rumble that seemed to shake the table, "Word is, Cross is killing his own guys if he so much as thinks they're talking. That makes him a wildcard."

I snorted quietly, half-smirking despite the headache. Black should've been doing movie trailers with a voice like that, not sitting in a clubhouse planning club politics.

Shadow nodded, his expression grim. "That makes him very dangerous. It's why we need to take this slow. The compound's prepped for a lockdown if it comes to that."

Viking leaned forward, his tone measured. "We can't jump the gun here. We don't know how many men he's got left or how much cash he's sitting on. It's not the right time to retaliate."

"Agreed," Vampire chimed in, his sharp features shadowed under the dim clubhouse lighting. "We wait this out. There's no rush."

Shadow glanced around the table, his gaze steady. "Black and West have connections in Philly now, so we're sitting tight for the moment. We'll move when we know more."

The shift in conversation was abrupt, and I could feel the air change as Stonewall asked, "What did you tell Mary about Carla?"

The room went quiet. We'd all agreed not to tell Mary the truth about Carla—about how Shadow had killed her. As far as Mary was concerned, the story cops fed the public was the truth: Carla had run off.

"I told her they found Carla's body yesterday. Overdose," Shadow said, his tone flat. "It'll put her mind at ease. She's been worrying too much."

Shadow's gaze swung to me. "Fuse, I need you to cover The Unlimited Friday and Saturday night. Viking's got things to take care of. Carl will close up, so you won't need to hang around long. Just make sure everything's running smooth."

"Sure thing, Shadow," I muttered. At this point, I'd have agreed to anything to get out of there. My skull felt like it was splitting in two.

"Any other business?" Shadow asked, glancing around the table.

No one spoke, and with that, Church was adjourned.

I pushed back my chair, my movements slow. I needed water, painkillers, and a bed—preferably in that order.

2

I walked into The Unlimited, the bass from the speakers already thrumming through the walls. The place was packed, just as Viking said it would be. A new band was playing tonight, and apparently, they were drawing a crowd.

Not that I cared about the music. I just wanted to check in and get out. There was a party back at the clubhouse, and that's where I really wanted to be. Maybe I could pick up some pussy from here to take back with me. The sweet butts weren't doing it for me lately—too predictable, too familiar.

I made my way to the bar, weaving through the crowd until I found an open stool. The warm buzz of voices mixed with the clink of glasses, creating a background hum that only amplified my headache from earlier.

"Hey, Fuse baby, what can I get you?" Tonya's voice cut through the noise as she leaned across the bar, giving me an eyeful of her abundant tits. Her tank top left nothing to the imagination, and she damn well knew it.

Without looking up from the tempting display, I said, "Whiskey, sweetheart."

She slid the glass over with a wink. "Anything else, baby?"

I knew exactly what she was offering. Tonya and I had been there, done that, and there was no round two. Civilians always took it as something more, and I wasn't about to deal with that drama.

"No, just here to check on things," I replied, keeping my tone casual.

I settled back with my drink, letting the whiskey burn down my throat as the band started to play. I hadn't bothered to look at the stage until now, but when I did, the air was punched right out of my lungs.

Holy. Fuck.

The lead singer was a knockout—gorgeous, fierce, and absolutely magnetic. And she was shredding an electric guitar like her life depended on it, belting out Metallica's "Sad But True." That song alone earned my attention. But her? She was something else entirely.

She was tiny, barely five-five and maybe a hundred and ten pounds soaking wet. Coal-black hair with sky-blue highlights framed a heart-shaped face, porcelain skin, and lips that could bring a man to his knees. Her eyes, the same electric blue as her hair, were rimmed with smoky makeup, giving her an edge that screamed "don't fuck with me".

And she was wrapped in leather. Tight, curve-hugging leather.

For the first time in my thirty years, I was stunned. Completely floored by a woman. The way she shredded that guitar, her fingers moving like lightning across the strings, had me mesmerized. Her face was animated, alive with the music. Every note she played seemed to pulse through her entire body, her energy electric and impossible to ignore.

I couldn't take my eyes off her. Hell, I didn't even want to. Then some guy on rhythm guitar ground himself against her during one of the songs, and I nearly cracked my glass in my hand. I didn't know where the hell that burst of jealousy came from, but there it was.

When the band finished their set, I downed the last of my drink and pushed off the bar. I had to meet her.

I made my way toward the stage, threading through the crowd like a man on a mission. But before I could get close, a familiar, high-pitched voice stopped me dead in my tracks.

"Fusie! Oh, Fusie, wait up!"

Shit. Kim.

I turned just in time to see her barreling toward me, her blonde curls bouncing as she shoved her way through the crowd. This was one of those moments where I seriously regretted not keeping it in my pants.

"Fusie baby! What a surprise!" she squealed, her voice grating against my already frayed nerves. "I didn't know you were here. Wanna go somewhere private and have some fun?"

She practically climbed on me as she spoke, her hands landing on my chest, her perfume choking the air between us.

I tried to keep it polite. "No, Kim. I've got things to do tonight. I'm working."

She pouted, sticking her lip out in an exaggerated attempt at looking cute. "Oh, boohoo. You always say that!"

"Well, it's the truth," I said, stepping back and peeling her hands off me. "I gotta roll."

Before she could trap me any further, I turned and headed for the stage. But when I got backstage, my heart sank. The singer was gone.

Most of their equipment was still here, though, which meant they were coming back for another set. I'd missed my chance for now, but I wasn't about to give up. Tomorrow night, I'd make damn sure I caught her.

For now, though, there was a party waiting for me, and I intended to enjoy it. The sun wouldn't be rising for hours, and I had plenty of time to make the most of the night.

3

After performing, it always took me a while to come down. The adrenaline coursing through my veins after a show was better than any drug. It was my high, my escape, the one thing in this world that made me feel truly alive. The rest of the band was crashing at a hotel in town, so after exchanging a round of goodbyes and "see you laters," I headed out.

This gig wasn't just about the music. I'd taken it to squeeze in a visit with my mom. It had been too long since I'd seen her, and I missed her more than I cared to admit. She was all I had left.

Shaylynn Alice Cooper, a party of one most of the time.

My dad was to thank—or blame—for the Alice Cooper part of my name. It was his idea of a joke, naming his daughter after the rock legend. Mom threw in "Shaylynn" to add a country flair, as if I was destined to prance around in a cowboy hat and rhinestones. But that wasn't my style. My life had always been more leather jackets and steel-toed boots than denim and daisies.

Still, being "a loner" didn't mean what it usually did. I had friends, sure. I partied, hung out, and even let people into my orbit from time to time. But letting someone truly close? No, thanks. I'd tried that once and got burned so badly I vowed never again.

As I walked to my car, my thoughts drifted back to earlier in the night. When I looked out into the crowd during our set, there was one face that stood out. One man who stared at me like he was utterly captivated. The intensity of his gaze sent a shiver through my body, even now.

He was gorgeous—unfairly so. Shoulder-length curly brown hair framed a chiseled face, complete with sharp cheekbones, a dimpled chin, and the kind of amber eyes that seemed to glow, cat-like, under the stage lights. For a second, I'd felt my heart stutter, the beginning of a connection.

And then I saw it. "The Devil's House" cut on his chest. That was the severing line, the point of no return. Whatever spark I thought I felt? Snuffed out, just like that.

I didn't date bikers. Period.

Especially not ones in an MC like "The Devil's House." My dad had been in that club, and I'd grown up watching what it did to my mom. Not abused, not neglected financially, but emotionally? My mom had been a shell of herself for years. Dad was always at the clubhouse, coming home drunk and reeking of other women. Mom used to cry in their bedroom at night, her sobs muffled by walls that couldn't quite contain the sound. Then one day—she didn't—just stop crying altogether. She just... accepted it.

I swore I never would.

One man had already tried to play me—keeping me while stringing along someone else on the side. I'd kicked his sorry ass out of my life the second I found out, and I never looked back. I'd rather spend my life alone than let a man treat me like that. Cheating, lying, and disrespect?

No way in hell.

As long as I had my music, my band—*Steel Stiletto*—I didn't need anything else. Music was my passion, my purpose. It was the only thing that truly belonged to me, and I wasn't about to let anything jeopardize that.

I threw my guitar into the backseat of my black 2015 Corolla and slid into the driver's seat. The car wasn't flashy, but it was mine, and it got me where I needed to go. Tonight, that was the clubhouse where mom lived. She'd stayed up waiting for me; I was sure of it. She always did, no matter how much I told her not to.

The drive gave me time to think. The moon hung low in the sky, casting a soft glow over the quiet streets. Memories of my mom's quiet strength and my dad's neglect ate at me as I navigated the familiar roads. My life might not be perfect, but at least I had control over it. I'd carved out a space for myself where no one could hurt me again, and I intended to keep it that way.

Still, I couldn't shake the image of the man in the crowd. That raw intensity in his eyes as he watched me perform. What was his story? Did he know who I was? Or was I just another pretty face under the spotlight to him?

Shaking my head, I dismissed the thought. It didn't matter. He was a biker, and I knew exactly where that road led. If there was one thing I'd learned from growing up in the shadow of an MC, it was this that their world wasn't meant for me.

I turned down the road that led to the clubhouse and smiled at the prospect as he let me through the gate, the light from the clubhouse glowing softly in the darkness. She'd be waiting inside, probably with a cup of tea and a million questions about the show. My heart softened at the thought. No matter how much I pushed people away, my mom always found a way to stay close.

Grabbing my guitar, I stepped out of the car and into the crisp night air. For now, I'd focus on what mattered—her. The rest of the world, and the man with the amber eyes, could wait.

4

When I got back to the clubhouse, the party was in full swing. The first bonfire since all that shit went down with Mary lit up the night, casting flickering shadows against the side of the building. Inside, the bar area buzzed with conversation and laughter, but it wasn't the kind of energy I was looking for.

Shadow, King, and Reader sat at the bar, their heads close as they talked business or something equally boring. I glanced around and spotted Mary with Jane and Lettie. Shadow's ol' lady was always close, like he couldn't stand to let her out of his sight. The man was obsessed, no doubt about it.

I gave the brothers a quick nod and tossed out a polite hello to the women as I grabbed a drink. The indoor crowd was tame—too tame. Shadow had decreed that the crazier shit stay outside, which was fine by me. I pushed through the doors and into the night, where the real party was raging.

Outside, it was a party, exactly what I needed. The bonfire roared in the center of the yard, surrounded by club members, women, and the usual brand of debauchery that came with our parties. I found an open seat next to Lord, who had one of the club girls, Jen, grinding on his lap. Her movements were exaggerated, meant to draw attention, but it was like he barely registered her presence.

Then, Lexi appeared out of nowhere, plopping herself right onto my lap like she belonged there, rubbing her tits on me. Her arms snaked around my neck as she leaned in close, her perfume cloying.

"Can Lexi take care of you, sweetie?" she purred, her voice syrupy as her hand went for my cock.

I grabbed her wrists and gently pushed her off me before I even realized what I was doing. She stumbled a bit, her eyes wide with surprise. Hell, I was just as surprised. What the fuck was wrong with me? Normally, I wouldn't have thought twice about letting her stay, but all I could see in my mind was *her*—the singer from the club.

Lexi leaned forward again, pressing her bare chest against me as she touched my face. "You okay, Fuse?"

Before I could answer, she appeared.

The singer.

She walked toward the clubhouse, her every step confident, her posture relaxed like she belonged here. She didn't so much as glance at the shit going on around her. Instead, her piercing blue eyes locked onto mine, and she smirked—a small, knowing expression that knocked the air out of my lungs. Then she disappeared inside.

What the fuck?

Why was she here? And what the hell was with that smirk, like she knew shit about me?

I jumped to my feet, muttering something to Lexi as I made my way toward the clubhouse. My drink was forgotten, and my pulse raced as I stepped through the doors, scanning the room. There she was, hugging Jane like they were old friends.

I stopped dead in my tracks, my mind spinning. What was I missing here? How did she know Jane?

I stayed where I was, watching from a distance. Up close, she was even more stunning. She was petite, almost delicate, but there was a strength in the way she carried herself. Everything about her was small—her nose, her breasts, even her boots—but she radiated a presence that couldn't be ignored. She wasn't my usual type, but something about her had me feeling like I'd stepped into the Twilight Zone.

Jane pulled away from their hug and started making introductions.

"Shay, you know Shadow, King, and Lettie," she said, gesturing to each of them in turn. "This lovely lady here is Mary, Shadow's ol' lady and fiancée. Over there are Reader and Black. And this here is Fuse." Jane pointed at me, her smile warm. "You can meet everyone else later."

Then she dropped the bomb.

"And for everyone here who doesn't know, this is Shay—my daughter. She's visiting for a bit."

Shay.

The name fit her. I rolled it around in my mind, liking the way it sounded, the way it suited her. Before I could process much more, I saw Black out of the corner of my eye. The way he was watching Shay set my teeth on edge. I knew that look—he was interested.

No fucking way.

Before he could make a move, I stepped in front of her, cutting him off. "I saw you play tonight, babe," I said, meeting her eyes. "You and your band are terrific."

Her eyes flicked up to mine for a brief moment before darting away. "Thanks. I'm glad you liked it," she said, polite but distant. She wasn't meeting my gaze, and her body language screamed that she was trying to keep her distance.

Interesting.

Women usually fell at my feet, but Shay was... different. She was attracted to me—I could tell—but she was fighting it. The challenge only made her more intriguing.

Black, the persistent bastard, chimed in, "You were the new band playing tonight? I'll have to make sure I catch your set tomorrow." He leaned casually against the bar, flashing his signature all-teeth grin that made women swoon.

I clenched my jaw. Black was the kind of guy women drooled over—sandy blond hair, golden eyes, and a physique that screamed rugged cowboy charm. But Shay wasn't going to fall for his act. Not if I had anything to say about it.

This one was mine. I just had to figure out why she was so hell-bent on resisting me.

I walked out to my car to grab my stuff, feeling the cool night air brush against my skin. I didn't need to turn around to know Fuse was behind me—I could feel his presence. I wished he would just stop.

I could tell he was interested; it was written all over him. But I knew men like him—smooth talkers, charmers, and heartbreakers. Fuse wasn't after anything more than sex—a one-night stand, and while I couldn't deny that I found him ridiculously attractive, I wasn't about to go down that road.

Especially not after seeing that sweet butt glued to him earlier.

"Hey, Shay, wait up. I want to talk to you," his voice called from behind me.

Damn. His voice. It was deep and smooth, like honey drizzling over gravel. I hated that I liked it so much.

I turned, keeping my face neutral. "What is it you want to talk about, Fuse?"

"As I said inside, I really enjoyed listening to you tonight. You and your band are incredible," he said, giving me a look I was sure he used on women every day—a combination of confidence and charm that probably made them melt. "So, I figured we could have a drink or something after your set tomorrow night."

I folded my arms, standing firm. "Look, Fuse, I'm sure you're a nice guy and all, and this is nothing personal. But I don't date bikers. Ever. Period."

His expression shifted, a flicker of curiosity crossing his face before his grin returned. "Why is that? You can't lump all bikers into one category and file us away as all the same. That's not fair. I might surprise you," he said, ending his statement with a wink.

I raised an eyebrow, unimpressed. "What I saw when I got here tonight is exactly why I don't date bikers. I grew up watching the same shitshow going on out back tonight—sweet butts on tap and partying. So, don't tell me I don't know. Or was I imagining that naked woman all over you earlier?"

Fuse's grin faltered slightly, and I pressed on.

"And you did that after you said you were interested in me, but that's what guys like you do. You want your cake and eat it too. And I'm not about to be dessert," I said, my tone sharp and unapologetic. I'd spent years learning to be upfront about what I wanted—and what I didn't.

He took a step back, his smirk twisting into something colder. "We're not all the same," he said, his voice tight. "But I guess if you believe that, who am I to change your mind? See you around, Shay."

With that, he turned on his heel and headed back toward the party.

I sighed, watching him go. I knew I'd pissed him off, but the truth hurt sometimes. Guys like Fuse always slept around—it was just who they were. Still, I couldn't deny that he was good-looking.

Frustratingly good-looking.

The worst ones always were.

Shaking my head, I reached into my car and grabbed my bag and guitar. I needed to focus on what mattered—getting inside and getting some sleep. Between traveling all day and performing tonight, I was running on empty.

As I walked back toward the clubhouse, I glanced up at the windows, hoping my room was far enough away from the party that I wouldn't hear it. The music and laughter would probably go until morning, but I needed quiet. My exhaustion weighed heavier with every step.

Once inside, I slipped down the hallway, my guitar case bumping gently against my leg. Tomorrow was a new day, and I had no intention of letting a man like Fuse—or anyone else—distract me from what I came here to do.

I was angry, and I couldn't even pinpoint why.

I didn't chase pussy—pussy chased me. Always had. So why the hell was I letting that little spitfire, Shay, crawl under my skin? I should've just walked away and forgotten about her the second she shot me down.

But I couldn't.

What pissed me off even more? She was right.

My life had been nothing but the club, women, and parties for as long as I could remember. That was the lifestyle I'd chosen, wasn't it? No attachments, no expectations, just living in the moment. Yet here I was, spiraling because one woman called me out on it.

I made my way back to the fire, where the party was still going strong. The flames flickered high into the night, casting shadows across the yard. Lord was slouched in his seat, his auburn hair a mess, green eyes glassy from whatever the hell he'd been drinking—or smoking.

"Where'd you wander off to?" he asked, his voice thick and slurred. "And why the hell did you turn down Lexi? You left her thinking she did something wrong."

I shrugged, sinking into my seat. "I'm just not feelin' it tonight. Been partying a lot lately—it's catching up with me," I said, keeping my tone light. No way in hell was I telling him the truth—that a mouthy woman had me rethinking my entire goddamn life.

Lord snorted, shaking his head. "You? Not feelin' it? That's a first. Have Lexi blow you while you smoke a joint—it'll relieve some stress. Then get some sleep."

I glanced toward the fire, where Lexi and Brooke were dancing, both completely naked. The firelight glinted off their skin, but instead of the usual reaction, I felt... nothing. Lexi caught my eye, and for a moment, something flickered there—something I didn't like.

Feelings.

Shit.

The women here knew the deal. They came to the parties for a good time, nothing more. Feelings weren't supposed to be part of the equation, and I prayed I was wrong about what I saw in Lexi's eyes. I wasn't interested in her like that.

Hell, right now, I wasn't interested in her at all.

"I think I'll head in alone and get some sleep," I said, standing and brushing the ashes from the fire off my jeans. "Might be coming down with something, feeling as run down as I do."

Lord gave me a skeptical look. "You? Sick? That's rich."

I ignored him, heading toward the clubhouse before he could press further. No way was I sticking around to let him rib me about acting soft—or worse, get into a conversation I wasn't ready to have.

Inside, the clubhouse was quieter than usual, the distant sound of music muffled by the walls. I headed straight to my room, shutting the door behind me and sinking onto the bed.

Sleep came quickly, but my dreams weren't peaceful. Shay's face haunted me, her smirk, her voice, the way she called me out without hesitation. She was a woman I couldn't escape, not even after I closed my eyes.

5

Getting up, I went through the motions of my morning routine—a quick shower, jeans, a T-shirt, and sneakers. I knew my mom well enough to know she'd have a breakfast spread waiting for me. As I opened the door and stepped out into the hall, the door next to mine opened, and out walked Fuse.

Of course. Of all the people to be my neighbor, it had to be him.

I tried not to stare, but damn, did he have to wear his jeans that tight? They left little to the imagination, and to my annoyance, I liked it. Hated myself for it, even.

"See something you like, Shay?" he said with a smirk, catching me mid-stare.

Shit. "I was zoning out, that's all," I said quickly. "Didn't expect you to be up this early—it surprised me."

His expression told me I wasn't convincing. The satisfied gleam in his eyes only made it worse.

"Are you headed to breakfast?" he asked, clearly enjoying my discomfort.

"Yeah. Mom probably cooked all my favorites," I replied, already starting down the hall. He fell into step beside me.

"That's where I'm headed too," he said casually, as if we hadn't just had an awkward moment.

We walked in silence, which felt both oddly comfortable and suffocating at the same time. When we reached the kitchen, the smell of bacon and fresh biscuits hit me, and I couldn't help but smile. Sure enough, my mom turned, her face lighting up.

"I made all your favorites, Shay. Blueberry pancakes, bacon, and homemade biscuits," she announced proudly.

No one made pancakes like my mom—fluffy, sweet, and packed with blueberries. My mouth watered as I grabbed a plate and piled it high before scanning the room for a seat. I chose a spot next to Shadow, Mary, and a man I didn't recognize.

"Good morning, Shay. Did you sleep okay?" Mary asked, her smile far too big for this early in the day.

"I actually slept really well. I was exhausted from traveling and playing," I admitted, taking a bite of my pancake.

"I'm happy to hear that. If you need anything, just let me know," she said, her smile warm and genuine.

She seemed too nice for Shadow, who had a reputation for being cold and unapproachable. "Thanks. I'll keep that in mind."

Before I could take another bite, the chair next to me scraped against the floor, and Fuse plopped down beside me. Great. Just great.

"Don't worry, I won't bite you... unless you want me to," he whispered in my ear, his voice low and teasing.

My body betrayed me, a shiver running down my spine. For fuck's sake. I had to be careful around Fuse—he was the kind of man who could undo all my carefully laid defenses. He was more attractive than any man I'd ever met, and that was dangerous.

Thankfully, the distraction of more people sitting across from us pulled my attention. Sweet Butts. Fantastic.

For the record, I don't have much use for them. And before you judge me, remember, these women sign up for this lifestyle knowing exactly what it entails. They don't care if the men they sleep with are married or not. And yeah, the men are to blame too—they all suck.

"Shay, this is Lexi and Brooke," my mom said, gesturing to the two women, "and I don't think you've met West yet."

The introductions went as expected. I muttered the usual pleasantries, but it was clear the brunette—Lexi—was sizing me up. Like I gave a shit. I was only being polite for my mom's sake.

That's when I felt it—a hand on my thigh.

I stiffened, glancing sideways. Fuse was eating his breakfast, not even looking at me, but his hand was unmistakable, creeping up my leg like it had every right to be there.

I jabbed him sharply in the ribs with my elbow, satisfied when he let out a grunt and sucked in a breath.

"Watch it, Loverboy, especially if you want to keep that hand," I hissed under my breath.

He leaned in slightly, his voice a low murmur. "Might be worth losing a hand to touch that pussy of yours."

I hadn't been expecting that. Heat flooded my face, and I realized, to my horror, that I was blushing. *Blushing.* I hadn't blushed since I was a teenager. How was this man making me, a twenty-eight-year-old woman, feel like an awkward schoolgirl?

I prayed no one noticed, but the scrape of a chair broke the moment. Lexi pushed her seat back with a loud thunk and stalked out of the room, her face twisted in something between anger and hurt.

Fuse didn't even glance her way, but I knew he'd seen. There was no way he hadn't. Lexi had it bad for him, and for some reason, that irritated me more than I wanted to admit.

After breakfast, I headed to the garage. When I wasn't out on club runs, this was my domain. I was a mechanic—and a damn good one. The garage, Smoke Auto Repair, was named after one of the founding club members and sat in the heart of downtown Hope Chapel. Along with Club Tattoo, which Stonewall ran, it was one of the two businesses the club owned in town.

The familiar smell of grease and oil wrapped around me as I stepped inside, the clang of tools and hum of engines filling the space. I should've been focused on the work, but my thoughts kept drifting back to this morning—and to Shay.

Being that close to her at breakfast, I could've gotten lost in her eyes alone. Those sharp blue eyes were mesmerizing, and the way she looked at me—like I was both an annoyance and a challenge—did something to me I couldn't explain.

I knew I should back off. She was determined not to give me the time of day, and for my own sake, I should take the hint. I wasn't exactly the commitment type. Hell, every woman who'd mattered to me had bailed—my mom, my sister, even my first two girlfriends. Women always left. That was my reality.

It was probably why I'd made it a rule to avoid anything serious since I was twenty. I didn't need the hassle of caring about someone just to watch them walk away.

But Shay... she was different.

She captured my attention the second I saw her on that stage, shredding her guitar like she owned the world. Meeting her only made it worse—her fire, her sass, her refusal to let me charm her like I did everyone else. It wasn't just her looks, though those didn't hurt. No, there was something about her that made me want her more than I'd wanted anything in a long time.

And this morning hadn't helped.

Fuck, she's sexy even when she was eating.

I hadn't noticed her tattoos last night because she'd been wrapped in leather from shoulder to toe. But seeing her in those tight jeans and a T-shirt, I couldn't miss them. One tat—a vine with dragonflies weaving through it—wrapped around her wrist and twisted up her arm before disappearing under her shirt. It made me wonder where it ended.

And yeah, it made me fantasize. A lot.

The woman was sexy as hell, no denying that. Even that sassy mouth of hers, which should've been a turn-off, just made me want her more.

I yanked my attention back to the car in front of me, wrench in hand, but it didn't last long. My thoughts veered toward Lexi. That little stunt she pulled this morning hadn't gone unnoticed. Everyone saw her storm out during breakfast, and that kind of shit drama didn't fly in the club. The sweet butts here knew the rules—no feelings, no expectations, no bullshit. I didn't give Lexi any more attention than the other women, so I had no idea where this was coming from.

I hated dealing with this kind of shit, but I'd have to talk to her. Clear the air. Lexi needed to understand her place before this spiraled into something bigger.

Still, my focus shifted back to Shay. No matter how hard I tried, I couldn't shake her. Tonight, I was going to The Unlimited to watch her sing again. I didn't have to be there, but fuck it—I couldn't resist. There was this pull I felt toward her, something I couldn't control.

I didn't know what it was about Shay, but I was hooked.

And yeah, I was probably fucked.

6

I spent the day hanging out with Mom, just talking and catching up. It felt good—I'd missed her more than I realized. Since Dad died four years ago from a heart attack, I'd worried about her constantly. But the club seemed to be keeping her busy, and she genuinely looked happy. That made me happy too. She deserved it.

Dad certainly never cared about her happiness, that's for damn sure.

By the time I walked into the nightclub, I was in a better mood than I'd been in a while. Heading straight to the back, I found Mark, Chris, and Gabe already there, tuning their instruments and setting up.

"You beat me here?" I asked, surprised. "I was sure you guys were hitting the strip club last night. Figured you'd be hungover."

Mark grinned, leaning on his guitar. "What can I say? We're professionals. Besides, not all of us went hard. Some of us have *class*," he teased, shooting Chris a look.

I rolled my eyes. "Right. Class. How's your head feeling this morning, Chris?"

Chris shrugged, grinning like the devil. "Head's fine. The rest of me? Satisfied."

"Gross," I said, laughing despite myself.

Mark turned his attention back to me. "Hey, how's your mom doing?"

I smiled at the mention of her. Mark was the band member I was closest to, my rock during some of the hardest times in my life—like when Shawn shattered me. Mark was there, no questions, just support. I loved all the guys, but Mark had a special place in my life. He was my Sebastian Bach for this era, a killer guitarist, an incredible singer, and not to mention hot. Not that I was interested—we were too much like family.

"She's doing great," I replied. "Keeping busy with the club. She'll be here tonight if you want to say hi after the show."

"Cool," Mark said with a nod. "I'll keep an eye out for her."

"I really thought I'd beat you guys here tonight," I said, crossing my arms. "Guess I underestimated you."

"Not all of us partied *too* hard," Mark said, smirking. "Some of us even got lucky."

"With women or each other," I shot back, giving him a skeptical look.

"Don't be jealous just because you can't have all this," Mark teased, flexing dramatically.

"In your dreams, buddy," I laughed, shooing him away. "Now go, I need to get ready."

As I changed into my stage outfit, my thoughts drifted to Fuse. I hadn't seen him at the club all day, and I couldn't help but wonder where he was—and why I cared. He was a biker, and I'd already told myself I wasn't going there. But my mind wasn't listening.

There was something about him that pulled at me. It wasn't just the physical attraction, though that was undeniable. There was something deeper, something I couldn't quite put my finger on. I hated how much space he was taking up in my thoughts.

Before I knew it, it was time to go on. Grabbing my guitar, I headed out onto the stage, the roar of the crowd greeting me. The bright lights warmed my skin, and for a moment, I let the music take over.

But then I saw him.

Sitting front and center, where I couldn't avoid him, was Fuse. Next to him were Mom, Shadow, Mary, and Black. My stomach did a little flip I wasn't prepared for. Fuse's intense gaze locked onto me, a small smirk playing on his lips like he knew exactly what kind of effect he had on me.

Just great.

I took a deep breath and gripped my guitar tighter, letting the weight of the instrument ground me. Tonight wasn't about him. It was about the music. That's what I told myself as I stepped up to the mic and let the first notes ring out. But the pull of his presence was impossible to ignore.

When I got to the club, I went straight for the table right in front of the microphone. I wanted to watch Shay perform up close—no distractions. Settling back, I waved over a waitress and ordered a drink. I barely had time to relax before I caught a group moving toward me out of the corner of my eye.

Shit.

It was Shadow, Mary, Jane, and Black. Heading straight for my table.

"Hey, Fuse, mind if we sit with you?" Shadow asked, though he didn't wait for an answer. He dropped into the chair next to me, pulling Mary onto his lap like she belonged there.

"I'm so excited to see my baby perform. I haven't seen her sing in years," Jane said, practically glowing with excitement. I glanced at her and noticed the resemblance to Shay for the first time—the same jet-black hair and petite build. But Shay's piercing blue eyes? She'd gotten those from her old man, no doubt about it.

The club was packed, as usual for a Saturday night, the steady hum of conversation and music filling the air. Then the DJ cut the music, and the lights dimmed. Shay and the rest of her band took the stage, and all that noise faded to a dull hum in the background.

Damn.

She was sexy as hell, dressed head-to-toe in leather that hugged every curve. When I finally got her into my bed—and I would—I'd peel that leather off her piece by piece, taking my time.

"She looks like a young Joan Jett. Sexy," Black muttered, eyes glued to the stage as the band kicked off their set.

I shot him a sharp look. This fucker better watch himself. They don't call me *Fuse* for nothing. I might look easygoing, but I could go from calm to dangerous fast when provoked. I wasn't the kind of man you threw sparks at unless you wanted to see what I could do.

The first song was sung by the other guitarist, with Shay on backup vocals. It was *Push* by Matchbox Twenty, but I barely heard him. I couldn't take my eyes off Shay. She was pure talent, her energy electric. The crowd loved her. *I* loved her, and that could be a problem.

The second song was hers. A slower one. *"Fading Like a Flower."* I didn't know it, but coming from her, it immediately became one of my favorites. Her voice was low and haunting, the kind of voice that stayed with you long after the music stopped.

I was so caught up in watching her that I barely registered the kick against my leg. I looked at Shadow, who gave me a subtle nod, signaling me to check my phone. Pulling it out, I saw the message:

Shadow: *Casually look to your right. The men sitting there have been watching us since we came in. They don't fit in.*

I waited a beat, then turned my head slightly. Two men sat a few tables away, their eyes locked on us. They didn't look local, and their stiff posture gave them away. They were trying to blend in, but they didn't belong. I took another quick glance, and the taller one caught my attention. Tattoos snaked up his neck—prison ink, gang-related.

Not good.

I typed a quick reply.

Fuse: *They're watching us for sure. Did you text Kickstand to log into the cameras and ID them?*

Shadow: *Yeah. He's on it. Stay after and make sure Shay gets back safe. I'm getting Mary and Jane out of here once Shay's set is done.*

I didn't reply, but I watched as Black got up and sauntered to the bar. Shadow had clearly sent him for a better angle to keep eyes on the men. Typical Shadow—always one step ahead.

I ran my hand down the side of my cut, feeling the familiar weight of my gun underneath. I hoped I wouldn't need it, but I wouldn't hesitate if things went sideways. You didn't live this life—*club life*—and hesitate when violence came knocking. I'd put down my fair share of men over the years. Am I proud of it? No. But I'm not ashamed, either. In this world, it's kill or be killed, and every man knows the stakes.

Turning my attention back to the stage, I froze when I saw Shay's eyes on me. For just a second, she looked straight at me before quickly averting her gaze. *Interesting.*

The other guitarist took the lead again, kicking off *"Bad Company"* by Five Finger Death Punch—one of my favorite songs. But I wasn't paying attention to him. I couldn't stop watching Shay. The way she moved on stage while she played—her hips swaying just enough to drive me insane—was too much.

Too fucking much.

I forced my focus back to the men, catching movement out of the corner of my eye. They were getting up to leave, and sure enough, Black wasn't far behind them. I knew Shadow had another brother waiting outside to follow them. Shadow didn't take chances, and tonight was no exception.

The band wrapped up their set, the applause thunderous, but I was already on my feet, weaving through the crowd. I wasn't about to let Shay slip past me tonight.

Heading backstage, I wasn't expecting to find Fuse leaning against the wall, looking completely relaxed—too relaxed—and dangerously handsome. His arms were crossed over his chest, the faintest smirk tugging at his lips like he'd been waiting for me. Part of me was surprised to see him back here. During the show, I'd caught moments where his attention seemed elsewhere, and I'd stupidly assumed he'd found a "plaything" for the night.

The idea didn't sit well with me. At all.

Fuse pushed off the wall and closed the space between us, his presence overwhelming in the small hallway.

"There's my sexy little rockstar," he said, his voice honey-smooth and full of promise, that sly smile of his making my stomach flip. "I've been charged with seeing you home safely."

I tilted my chin up, refusing to let him get the upper hand. "Why would you—or anyone—need to see me home? I'm a big girl, Fuse. I can manage just fine on my own."

"Big?" he said, his amber eyes glinting with mischief. "You're tiny, little rockstar. I could fit you in my pocket... or down the front of my jeans. Your choice."

His teasing words sent heat rushing to my face. I scowled, willing myself to stay calm. "Knock it off, Fuse." My voice was steady, but I hated how his nickname for me made something flutter low in my stomach. I had to be careful. He could wear me down, and I wasn't about to let that happen.

He grinned, unbothered. "Oh, Shay, I'm sure if I reached into those tight leather pants of yours, I'd find your panties wet. Shall we find out?"

"Stop it, Fuse," I snapped, swatting his hand away when he reached for me. "Just tell me why you think you need to see me home. I told you—I'm fine."

His smirk faded, replaced by something more serious, though the glint of playfulness never fully left his gaze. "Shadow ordered it. That's all you need to know. And no, I can't tell you why—it's club business."

I stiffened at that. *Club business.* Growing up around the club, I knew exactly what that phrase meant: danger. Something—or someone—was a threat. I wanted to push for answers, but I also knew how tight-lipped bikers could be. If Shadow said I needed an escort, it wasn't just for fun.

Fuse's voice softened slightly, as if sensing my hesitation. "But listen, I was planning to catch up with you after the show anyway. So, I figured we could go back to the clubhouse, have a drink, and talk."

Talk?

That sounded dangerous for entirely different reasons.

Here was where I hated myself. I wanted to spend time with Fuse. I shouldn't, and I wasn't ready for more with him, but something about him made me want to know him—the real him, if that even existed. He was infuriating, cocky, and way too confident for his own good. And yet, I was drawn to him, like ants to sugar.

I sighed, feeling like I was walking straight into trouble. "Fine. But if I agree to a drink with you, it doesn't mean sex. Understand me, Fuse?"

His grin returned, slower this time, as if he knew he'd won something. "Of course, my little rockstar. Whatever you're comfortable with. I won't push it further than what you're willing to give me... for now anyway."

I narrowed my eyes at him. "For now?"

"Hey, I'm just being honest," he said, holding up his hands like he was innocent. "A man can hope."

"Since I have my car, you'll have to follow me back," I said, ignoring the butterflies in my stomach as I slung my guitar case over my shoulder.

Fuse didn't argue. "Fair enough."

I pushed through the back door of the nightclub, the cool night air hitting me as I stepped outside. Fuse was right behind me, his footsteps steady and confident. I didn't look back, but I could feel his presence close enough to make my skin tingle.

This was a mistake. I knew it.

But for some reason, I couldn't make myself stop.

7

I followed Shay back to the clubhouse, feeling like I was finally making progress. *Finally*. She'd agreed to have a drink with me and talk. With Shay, I knew I had to take things slow—one wrong move, and she'd shut me out completely. I didn't want to overthink why I wanted her so damn badly or what it meant, but there it was.

When we pulled into the clubhouse lot, the party was in full swing out back—music, laughter, and the low roar of conversation filling the night air. Normally, I'd be drawn to it, but tonight, I couldn't care less. The only thing on my mind was Shay. I parked my bike and headed for her car. She was getting out, slinging her guitar case over her shoulder. I waited for her, matching her steps as we walked inside together.

"Grab me a whiskey sour," she said over her shoulder, already halfway up the stairs. "I'll put my guitar in my room and be right back."

"Got it," I called after her, watching her go. Damn, even walking away, she was something else.

I headed into the bar area, which was a rowdier scene than last night. Brothers were shooting pool, tossing back drinks, and dancing with the club girls as music blasted from the speakers. The air was thick with smoke and laughter, but I ignored the calls and nods from others as I made my way to the bar.

"Whiskey and a whiskey sour, prospect," I said, motioning to the kid behind the bar. When he handed me the drinks, I took them to a quieter corner, finding a table with enough space for Shay and me. I ignored a few more attempts to pull me into conversation and sank into the chair, waiting.

For a second, I worried Shay might ditch me. Maybe I'd pushed her too hard already. But when I saw her walking back into the room, I relaxed. She was still in her leather pants and boots, looking every bit the rockstar she was. Her light blue eyes locked on me, and I had to focus to keep from staring too long. She looked damn good.

Shay slid into the seat across from me, her posture relaxed but her expression guarded. "First things first," she said, grabbing her drink. "What's your real name? If we're going to talk, I'm not calling you by your road name."

I smirked. "Scott Jackson. Haven't heard it in years, though."

"Scott," she repeated, like she was testing it out. "I like it. It fits you."

I grinned. "And what's your full name, little rockstar?"

She grimaced like I'd struck a nerve. "Shaylynn. Don't laugh—I hate it. I only go by Shay."

"Shaylynn sounds like a country singer or something," I teased. "But Shay suits you better."

She didn't laugh this time. Instead, she studied her drink, her fingers absently tracing the rim of the glass. "My dad loved the name. Said it sounded soft and pretty, but I never really liked it," she said quietly. "My mom calls me Shay, so that's what I go by."

Something in her voice gave me pause, but I let it go—for now. "So, Shay, how long have you been playing the guitar?"

She seemed grateful for the shift in conversation. "I started playing when I was around twelve. I used to watch music videos, completely enamored with the guitar players. I begged my parents for lessons until they finally caved. I've been playing ever since. I met my bandmates about seven years ago, and we've been together ever since."

"You're good," I said honestly, tipping my glass toward her. "Cool as hell shredding that guitar. How come I haven't seen you around here before this week? I've been with the club eight years now, and I damn well would've remembered meeting you."

Shay's lips quirked up into a half-smile. "I left when I was eighteen. I wanted out."

"Out?" I frowned. "Why?"

She looked at me, her gaze steady and unflinching. "Because I hated everything about club life back then. My dad was part of this club, and I watched what it did to my mom. He wasn't a bad man—not to me, at least—but he was a biker through and through. Always gone, always coming home drunk, smelling like cheap perfume. My mom spent years crying herself to sleep until she just... stopped. She accepted it. That was her life."

Her voice softened, but the bitterness underneath was clear. "I couldn't stand seeing her like that. And I knew if I stayed, I'd end up the same—stuck, miserable, waiting for a man who cared more about the club than his family. So I left. I moved around a lot at first, trying to figure out where I belonged, but I settled in Baltimore when the band formed. It was the first place that felt like mine."

I stayed quiet, letting her words settle between us. I knew exactly what she was talking about. The club had been a mess back then—bad leadership, no respect, nothing but chaos. Shadow had turned things around since then, but I couldn't blame her for running.

"The club's not like it used to be, Shay," I said finally. "Shadow runs a tighter ship. It's not perfect, but it's better—your mom would probably agree."

"She does," Shay admitted. "She says things have changed. But you can't convince me men have. You get enough booze and women in front of them, and they give in. My dad did it to my mom, and I know damn well he wasn't the only one."

I sighed. I couldn't argue with her there. "Fair point, but it doesn't apply to all of us."

Shay leaned back in her chair, a flicker of something softer crossing her face. "So, Scott," she said, deliberately lightening the mood, "what else do you do besides play Road Captain? Work at the garage, right? Somehow, I can't picture you turning wrenches."

I smirked, grateful for the shift. "You can stop by and see for yourself, little rockstar. Maybe while you're there, I'll check under *your* hood, see what makes you run."

Her laugh was low and husky, sending heat straight through me. "Scott, you couldn't handle what I've got under my hood. You're used to the easy women around here. You wouldn't know what to do with me."

"Is that a challenge?" I asked, leaning closer. "Because if it is, I'm all in."

Her baby blues flashed, and I knew she was about to fire back when an unwelcome voice cut in.

"Here you are, Fuse." Lexi's sultry tone made my teeth grind. I looked up to see her sauntering toward us, her fake pout already in place. "I waited for you outside, baby. You've been hiding in here?"

Before she could pull one of her stunts, she put her hands on my shoulders and leaned in far too close. I shoved her back gently but firmly, glaring at her.

"Get lost, Lexi," I said coldly, my voice like steel.

She pouted, but finally backed off. The damage, however, was done. I turned back to Shay just in time to see her pushing away from the table. Her expression was tight, her shoulders stiff.

"Shay—wait."

She didn't stop, and I caught up to her in the parking lot just as she was pulling open her car door.

"Why did you run off?" I asked, trying to keep my voice calm. "Lexi was out of line. You shouldn't let her get to you."

Shay turned on me, her blue eyes blazing. "Are you for *fucking real?* If I hadn't been sitting there, would she have been out of line? No, Scott. You'd have taken whatever she was offering."

"That's not true," I said firmly. "I can keep my cock in my pants,

Shay. I like you, and I was enjoying hanging out with you."

Before she protest, I pressed my lips onto hers, catching her off guard as I made my intentions clear. She surrendered in what felt like mere seconds, her tongue dancing with mine as we devoured each other. I pulled her body closer to mine, lifting her up and wrapping her legs around my waist as I pushed my hard cock into her stomach. Her hands traveled through my hair, pulling at the strands as she rotated her hips against me.

But just when things were reaching a fever pitch, the door across the hallway flung open and Stonewall emerged. The sight of him was enough to snap us out of our trance and Shay quickly pushed me away, retreating into her room without a word.

"Your timing fucking sucks," I grumbled, shooting a scowl at Stonewall.

"Sorry man, how was I supposed to know you were trying to fuck outside my door? Wait...was that Shay?" he asked, raising an eyebrow in surprise.

"Yeah, what about it? How do you know her?" My jealousy was rising again, unable to control my possessiveness.

"I've known her since we were kids. She's older than me, but I remember her. Saw her a few years ago when her old man passed away," Stonewall explained. "Chill the fuck out. I get enough of that shit from Shadow."

"I'm just touchy since I was about to get lucky, and I was feeling it good, if you get me?" I said, trying to brush off my jealousy.

"Don't screw around with Shay unless you're serious about her. If all you want is pussy, you should just leave her alone. Jane will kill you if you hurt her. And trust me, Shadow is not gonna be happy either," Stonewall warned me.

"Can everyone stop assuming that all I care about is getting laid? Has anyone considered that maybe I actually like Shay?" I snapped back defensively, unsure of why I felt the need to defend myself.

"Everyone assumes that because that is you, Fuse. You love women and you don't hide it. So just think twice before messing with Shay if you're not gonna treat her right. Now I'm off to the party. See you at Church tomorrow," Stonewall said before walking away, leaving me alone with my thoughts.

I stood outside Shay's door for a moment, contemplating whether or not to knock and try to talk things out with her. But ultimately, I decided to wait until morning and went to my room.

But I couldn't sleep. The frustration and anger over being interrupted boiled inside me, so I grabbed the bottle of Jack I kept hidden in my room and drowned my feelings in alcohol until unconsciousness finally claimed me.

I pressed my ear against the door, barely breathing as I strained to hear Fuse's voice. He was talking to Stonewall, and I knew I shouldn't eavesdrop, but I couldn't help it. I *needed* to know what he was thinking. The way Fuse looked at me, the way he'd touched me earlier, had me spinning in circles, and I was desperate for answers I couldn't just ask for outright.

My heart did a little flip in my chest as I continued to listen to the men, my pulse quickening, even as I pressed my hand against the door to steady myself.

"Careful with Shay," Stonewall replied, his tone calm but firm, warning him about my mom and stuff.

Fuse sighed, a sound heavy enough to make my stomach drop and then smiling to myself when he said it wasn't just about getting laid, only to lose that smile a second later.

"Everyone assumes that because that is you, Fuse.," Stonewall shot back, almost teasing, but there was truth beneath the words. "You love women and you don't hide it. So just think twice before messing with Shay if you're not gonna treat her right. Now I'm off to the party. See you at church tomorrow."

I squeezed my eyes shut. My fingers curled into my palm as if I could grab hold of the words and stop them from sinking in. Stonewall's warning hit the mark. It confirmed my deepest fear: Fuse was a player, the type who collected women like trophies and moved on when the shine wore off. I could picture him with Lexi or any of the other sweet butts—easy, willing, and completely fine with being one and done.

Not me. I can't do that.

I lingered as the conversation trailed off, the sound of boots against the wood floor letting me know Stonewall was walking away. My heartbeat picked up again. Would Fuse follow him and head to the party? I held my breath, straining to hear any sign of movement. For a long, agonizing moment, there was nothing. Then I heard his door creak open, pause, and quietly shut again. Relief washed over me. He wasn't going to the party. He was going to his room instead.

I exhaled, finally stepping away from the door. My legs felt shaky, as though holding myself there had drained the strength from them. I didn't know why I cared so much, but it mattered. It mattered that he wasn't going out to find comfort in someone else.

Dragging myself into the bathroom, I changed into a pair of soft cotton shorts and a tank top. The cool fabric brushed against my skin, soothing me as I climbed under the covers. My thoughts, however, were far from calm.

Fuse.

I couldn't stop thinking about him. My mind rewound to earlier, to the way he had me pinned against the door, his face so close, his breath hot against my skin. The memory alone sent a flush creeping up my neck. I wasn't going to lie to myself—he made me *hot as hell*. His lips on mine, the way his strong hands gripped my waist like I was something precious... I'd never felt anything like that before. And when his amber cat eyes glowed in the dim light, they made him seem almost *otherworldly*, like he was something more than just a man.

If we hadn't been interrupted, how far would I have let it go? My stomach tightened as I turned onto my side, the sheets twisting around me. I knew the answer. I would have let him take me as far as he wanted, and that terrified me. I'd spent years guarding my heart, building walls that no man had managed to scale—until Fuse.

Then there was *Lexi*. The way she'd walked up to us earlier, bold as you please, her skin on full display like she knew she belonged there. That confidence told me everything I needed to know—Lexi had been with Fuse before, and she was sure she could have him again. Just another woman in a long line of club girls who didn't mind sharing.

I can't live like that. I couldn't be part of a relationship in this kind of environment—it was toxic. I'd grown up watching my mom cry herself to sleep more nights than I could count, waiting for my dad to come home. I'd seen the destruction firsthand, and I swore I'd never let myself fall into the same trap.

I'm not the type of woman to be used and tossed aside. I want more. I deserve more.

So why, even knowing what I know, does Fuse make me feel this way? Why does he make me second-guess everything I've worked so hard to protect?

I flipped onto my other side with a frustrated sigh, the cool pillow pressing against my cheek. The truth was, this... whatever it was with Fuse... was the closest I'd come to being tempted in years. It scared me more than anything. Trust didn't come easy for me—not after what I'd seen growing up, and not after what I'd experienced for myself.

The thought of letting someone in, letting *him* in, was enough to send me spiraling. What would I do if I fell for him and he proved Stonewall right? If Fuse really was a player, and I became just another name he could forget?

No. I couldn't let that happen. I wouldn't.

Still, as I stared up at the ceiling, the sound of the party outside drifting through the open window, I couldn't stop the feeling that Fuse was different. There was something there—something I couldn't explain—that made me want to take the risk.

For now, though, I needed to protect myself. I couldn't let myself get caught up in his charm, his teasing, or the way his eyes seemed to see through all my defenses. I wouldn't be that girl, no matter how much he tempted me.

Finally, exhaustion started to pull me under, my thoughts

growing fuzzier by the second. Fuse's voice lingered in my head, low and smooth as honey, his words replaying like a song I couldn't shake.

"I'm not going to fuck this up."

I wanted to believe him. God help me, I *wanted* to.

But trust? That was something Fuse would have to earn.

8

I woke up with a splitting headache. *Why do I do this to myself?* I knew exactly what would happen when I drank like that—nothing good. Groaning, I sat up and rubbed my temples before reaching for the bottle of painkillers on the nightstand. I downed two pills with the lukewarm water I'd left sitting there, wincing as I swallowed. My stomach churned, threatening rebellion at the thought of food.

Shit. I had church in an hour.

Dragging myself into the shower, I let the cold water hit me first, jolting me awake. The pounding in my head softened slightly as I stood there, hands braced against the tiles, water cascading down my back. Eventually, I forced myself out, dried off, and dressed quickly—jeans, boots, and my cut. I ran my fingers through my damp hair, gave up on making it look decent, and walked out of my room.

As I passed Shay's door, I hesitated. The hallway was silent, but I couldn't help myself—I leaned in just a little, trying to hear if she was inside. *Nothing.* She was probably already at breakfast. The thought of food made my stomach lurch again, but at least I didn't have to face her yet. I wasn't sure what the hell I'd say to her after yesterday.

With five minutes to spare, I walked into the meeting room for church. Most of the brothers were already there, lounging back in their chairs, cigarettes burning in their hands. Stonewall rolled in just after me, looking about as hungover as I felt. We exchanged a brief nod before taking our seats.

Shadow, ever the hard-ass when it came to schedules, started the meeting right at ten. The man was a stickler for control—it was one of the things that made him a great president but also made him a prime target for being messed with from time to time.

"Alright," Shadow said, his voice sharp as he looked around the room. "We seem to have a problem. Last night at the nightclub, I noticed two men watching our table. I knew right away they weren't there for the nightlife." His gaze shifted to me and Black. "Fuse, Black, and I all agreed something was off. Kickstand's working on identifying them. Black and Vampire followed the guys after they left. I'll let Vampire fill us in."

Vampire leaned forward, resting his forearms on the table. "Once the men left the nightclub, Black and I tailed them—kept our distance to avoid spooking them. They ended up at a rundown shithole outside of town. Real piece of work. Around a half-hour later, a couple of what looked like hookers showed up. They stayed there the rest of the night. West's on watch now. So far, no new activity."

Black added in his deep rumble, "These guys are gang-related—no doubt about it. They weren't just watching us for fun. It looked like they were taking mental notes. Patterns, numbers, potential weaknesses they could use."

Viking leaned back, his face tight with concern. "Shadow, have you thought any more about lockdown? You had Mary, Jane, and Shay there last night. If those guys are scouting us, they could use the women against us."

At the mention of Mary, Shadow's expression darkened. Everyone knew how protective he was of her—sometimes borderline obsessive. "I know, Viking," he ground out. "I thought about that all damn night. Punched the hell out of the bag in the gym over it, too." He exhaled sharply, forcing himself to calm down. "We'll go on lockdown if we need to. At the very least, we'll bring the women and kids here."

Moreno spoke up. "I'll be the first to bring my old lady and kids in. Joe can homeschool them for a while—it's safer that way. King?"

"Same here," King replied. "Lettie's going to fight me over it—she's got her job at the salon—but she'll do as I say when it comes to safety."

"What about you, Soldier?" Shadow turned his gaze toward him. "Will Mandy come here?"

Soldier shrugged, but there was tension in his face. "Depends if she can get leave from work. But if it comes down to it, and I think she's in danger, I'll make it happen."

Soldier was so fucking strange when it came to Mandy. Brother loved her, she was sweet and pretty. I couldn't understand why he fucked around on her. Not often but he did.

Shadow nodded, clearly satisfied for now. "Vampire, keep your eyes open at the strip club and any of our other businesses. If someone doesn't fit or acts suspicious, I want to know."

"Will do," Vampire replied. "Any updates on the Fire Dragons' operations?"

Shadow shook his head. "Not much. Cross is keeping everything locked down tight. The guys we're watching might be our way in, though. If it turns out they're spying, we'll bring them in and get answers."

Shadow shifted gears, looking at me. "We've got a run to Florida coming up. Two weeks long. Domino, Runner, and Johnny will handle it. Fuse, you'll set everything up for their ride down and back. Think you can leave Shay alone long enough to do that?" he added with a smirk.

I shot him a middle finger, smirking back. "Funny, asshole. I'll take care of it."

Shadow ignored me, looking toward Stonewall. "Don't forget, I'm bringing Mary by tomorrow for her tattoo. Is the design ready?"

Stonewall nodded. "Yeah, it's done. It says, 'I Belong to Shadow,' but I worked Mary's name into the design, too. I'll show it to you after the meeting."

I snorted to myself. Shadow might as well just piss all over Mary with his possessiveness. I used to think it was overkill, but now, after meeting Shay, I kind of got it.

Viking leaned forward. "Reminder—we're going on a ride today. Up into the mountains, stopping for drinks, and heading back. It's a beautiful day to be out."

"Any other business?" Shadow asked, scanning the room. When no one spoke, he nodded. "Meeting adjourned."

The room erupted into noise as brothers stood and chairs scraped against the floor. But I wasn't paying attention anymore. My mind had already shifted to Shay. I wondered if I could persuade her to ride with me today. The thought of her on the back of my bike, arms wrapped around me, her body pressed against my back—it was enough to get my blood pumping.

Yeah, I thought, pushing out of my chair. *I need to find her. And I need to convince her to come with me.*

9

Walking into the kitchen, I found a few of the women milling around alongside some of the men, laughter and the scent of bacon filling the air. But the biggest surprise was my mom—dressed in her riding leathers. *Her riding leathers.* I froze, blinking as if I'd imagined it.

"Mom?" I said, frowning in disbelief. "Are you going on the ride?"

She turned to me with a grin that made her look years younger, her cheeks flushed. "You betcha, baby girl. I'm riding with Silver today."

Silver?

I tried not to look shocked, but the thought of my mom back on a bike—and with Silver, of all people—caught me off guard. Silver had been part of the club forever, an old friend of my dad's. He was a good guy, but still... my mom hadn't ridden since Dad died.

"Really?" I said slowly, processing. "That's great, Mom."

"You should come along, sweetie," Lettie chimed in from behind me. "It'll be fun."

I turned to Lettie, trying to bow out gracefully. "That's okay. I don't want to put anyone out by riding on the back of their bike."

Lettie rolled her eyes. "Get real, Shay. Half the guys here would *love* to have a hot chick like you on the back of their bike."

Before I could argue, a deep, familiar voice cut in, smooth as honey. "And here's one guy who would definitely love to have a hot chick like our little rockstar on his bike."

I turned just in time to see Fuse walking up, looking unfairly tempting. His shirt stretched over tattooed arms, the sleeves rolled up just enough to showcase the ink snaking up his skin. And those jeans... *damn.* They fit him like a second skin. Then there was that smile of his —wicked and confident—aimed straight at me. My heart stuttered, and I hated myself for how easily he got under my skin.

"See? It's settled," my mom said, practically beaming. "You're coming along today, Shay."

"Mom..." I tried one more time. "I don't want to impose on Fuse. He might already have someone riding with him."

"Nope." Fuse's amber eyes glinted with satisfaction. "The seat's empty, little rockstar. Go get changed, and I'll get my bike ready for the ride."

And just like that, he turned on his heel and walked out, leaving me no room to argue. I stared after him, my pulse racing as the room fell into a knowing silence. Lettie smirked at me like she could see every thought I was trying to hide.

"Fine," I muttered, grabbing a quick bite to eat before heading upstairs. I couldn't argue with Mom—she looked too excited about the idea of us both riding. And if I was being honest with myself, the thought of getting back on a bike stirred something in me. It had been years—since I was eighteen, to be exact—and I'd forgotten how much I loved the feel of the wind and the road beneath me.

But riding behind *Fuse*? That was going to be a test. A test I wasn't sure I'd pass.

After changing into fitted jeans, boots, and a tank top, I grabbed my leather jacket and headed outside. The lot was full—close to thirty bikes lined up for the run, their chrome glinting under the morning sun. I scanned the crowd until I spotted Fuse, leaning casually against his bike near the back. His Harley Softail was painted a deep, blood-red with black skulls. Not cartoonish or silly—*menacing*. These skulls looked like they belonged in nightmares, the kind of paint job that screamed *danger* and suited Fuse perfectly.

He looked up as I approached, his smile slow and lazy, like he'd been expecting me. "Ready, Shay?"

"As ready as I'll ever be." I ran my hand along the edge of his bike, pretending to inspect it. "You sure you know what you're doing, though? I'd hate to ride with a guy who can't handle his machine."

Fuse's grin turned downright sinful as he leaned closer, his voice dropping to a low murmur near my ear. "Oh, I know what I'm doing, baby. I ride fast and hard—just like I fuck."

Before I could think better of it, I shot back, "Both remain to be seen, Fuse. You could just as easily be like a biker who pulls out without looking to see if someone's coming."

His amber eyes flared with amusement. "Challenge accepted, little rockstar." He handed me a helmet with a wink before pulling on his aviators and strapping on his own. "Hop on. Hold tight."

God help me.

Swinging my leg over, I settled onto the back of his bike, careful to keep my hands on his sides instead of wrapping my arms around him. Fuse, of course, had other ideas. He grabbed my hands and pulled them firmly around his waist, forcing my chest against his back. My breath hitched, and I knew I should pull away—but I didn't. It felt too good. *Too right.*

The rumble of the engine beneath us sent a shiver through my body as Fuse started the bike and pulled up alongside Shadow at the front of the pack. Shadow gave a nod, and with that, they took off, the rest of us falling into formation behind them.

As we hit the open road, the wind rushed past, tugging at my hair and filling my lungs with air that smelled like freedom—like asphalt, leather, and the faint scent of Fuse's cologne. He rode exactly as he promised—fast and hard. The bike leaned into every curve with precision, the sudden dips and turns making my stomach tighten and my adrenaline spike. I couldn't stop the smile that spread across my face. *I'd forgotten how much I loved this.*

I pressed my cheek against his cut, feeling the worn leather beneath my skin. Fuse blocked most of the wind, his strong frame shielding me, and for the first time in a long time, I let myself relax. There was something about riding—about the hum of the engine and the stretch of the open road—that felt raw and wild. Untouchable.

I held on tighter, letting the bike carry us wherever Fuse wanted to go. For now, I wasn't going to think about the consequences or the chaos he brought into my life. For now, I was just going to enjoy the ride.

I liked this feeling—Shay on the back of my bike. I never took passengers unless it was absolutely necessary, and *never* a woman. They always took it the wrong way, thought it meant something more. But Shay didn't know this wasn't normal for me, and I wasn't about to tell her. She wouldn't have come if she'd known.

But already, I knew Shay was different. Special.

The harder I rode, the tighter she held on to me, her small hands clinging to my stomach like she belonged there. It made something shift inside me, something I couldn't name. So, naturally, I pushed my bike harder, leaning into the curves and eating up the road like I had something to prove.

As Road Captain, I knew we were getting close to our first stop—a biker bar that sat on the edge of a lake. It was a regular stop for the club, a place we knew well. Slowing down, I signaled the group and led them into the gravel parking lot. Engines rumbled and died one by one as brothers parked their bikes, laughing and calling out to each other.

I shut off my bike and waited, watching as Shay slid off. She removed her helmet and shook her hair loose, running her fingers through it as if to fix the helmet's damage. I couldn't stop staring. Even with her sunglasses hiding her baby blues, she was gorgeous—*too* gorgeous.

"So," I said, smirking as I leaned against my bike. "What'd you think? Hard enough for you, Shay?"

She grinned, and damn, that smile hit me square in the chest. "I could lie to you, but I won't. I loved it. It was exciting. I haven't ridden in forever."

"Now just imagine me fucking you the same way—hard and fast." I leaned in close, my voice low, and blew gently against her ear. Satisfaction shot through me when I saw the shiver ripple down her spine.

Before she could respond, our moment was interrupted by Silver and Jane walking up. Silver had been out of the pen for a month, and since his release, his attention had been all on Jane. Most brothers hit the Clubhouse hard when they got out, taking advantage of the parties and the women, but not Silver. Jane was it for him, and it was obvious.

"Good ride, Fuse?" Silver asked with a knowing grin.

"Best one yet," I replied, shooting a glance at Shay, who pretended not to hear.

The brothers headed inside, but I wanted Shay to myself. Taking her by the elbow, I gently steered her toward the bar, where we ordered drinks. Once we had them, I led her outside to a quiet table overlooking the lake. The sunlight hit the water, making it glitter like glass, the occasional splash from fish breaking the stillness.

"I love this place," Shay said, her voice soft as she gazed out over the lake. "It's beautiful. I didn't even know this was here."

"The club's been stopping here for years. It's a good place to take a break, get your head straight. And it's quiet enough for a conversation." I paused, holding her gaze. "Like the one we were having last night."

Shay took a sip of her drink and raised an eyebrow at me. "Alright, I'm game. Why'd you join the club?"

I set my glass down, turning slightly in my chair to face her. "When I turned eighteen, I left home to get away from my old man. He was a mean drunk—one of those guys who thought fists were the only way to handle things. So I took off. Moved around for a while, got into trouble. I was just a punk kid back then, looking for a fight everywhere I went."

I ran a hand through my hair, memories flickering like a reel in my head. "One night, when I was nineteen, I ended up at a biker bar looking for trouble. I was acting like an ass, mouthing off, ready to throw punches. That's when this guy in a *Devil's House* cut sat me down. His name was Hoss. He didn't beat the shit out of me like I probably deserved. Instead, he talked to me. Asked me why I was hellbent on getting myself killed."

"Hoss," Shay murmured, her expression softening. "I remember him. He used to give me candy when I came around the Clubhouse as a kid. What happened to him?"

"He sponsored me into the club a year later. Taught me everything I know. Then, a year after I got my patch, he died. Hit head-on by a truck while he was on a run." I paused, staring at the water. "He was a better man to me than my old man ever was."

Shay's voice was gentle. "I'm sorry. That's a terrible way to go. But I guess... in this life, you'd want to go out on your bike, doing what you love."

"Exactly," I said, nodding. "Better that than wasting away somewhere."

I cleared my throat and shifted the focus. "My turn. How long are you staying this time, Shay? When are you moving on?"

Her lips curved faintly, like she wasn't sure what to make of the question. "Well, we agreed to play at *The Unlimited* for a month. After that, we've got a gig lined up in Pittsburgh, and then the band's taking a break for a while. Mark usually lines up our gigs, so I don't know where we're headed next."

"So you'll be at the club with your mom for three months?" I asked, trying to keep my tone casual. Inside, though, relief washed over me like a wave. Three months. I had three months with her.

"Yeah, that's the plan. Mom and I were due for some time together. This worked out perfectly."

Hell yes. I didn't let myself think too hard about why I was so damn glad to hear that. I just was.

My phone buzzed on the table. I glanced down, frowning when I saw a message from Shadow. "I need a word. Out front."

"Everything okay?" Shay asked, watching me.

"Shadow wants to talk. You might want to hit the restroom before we head out again." I stood and walked her toward the building, making sure the area was clear of any assholes. As we got closer, I spotted her mom and some of the other women heading that way. That made me feel better about leaving her.

Once she was safely inside, I stepped out front and found Shadow waiting with Viking, Vampire, and Stonewall. The tension was thick, and I knew immediately something was wrong.

"What's up?" I asked.

Shadow handed me his phone, showing me a picture of a truck. "West says the men from the hotel followed us here. They're parked just down the road, waiting for us to leave."

Vampire crossed his arms. "Sounds like we've got a rat. How else would they know where we were headed?"

"Exactly," I said, scowling. "That grill on the front of that truck? They could plow through us from behind if they wanted to."

Shadow's expression was hard. "We need answers, but we can't do anything here with the women around. Here's the plan—we ride back, let them follow us. Viking, Stonewall, and Vampire, you'll break off in town, tail them, and take care of it. Wound them if you have to, just don't kill them yet."

"And the rat?" I asked.

"We'll handle that back at the Clubhouse. From now on, church business stays between the brothers who usually attend. My money's on a new patch or a prospect."

The door opened, and I saw Shay walking toward me. I forced myself to relax, pushing the tension aside as she smiled faintly, heading my way. God, she was pretty. Too pretty.

She stopped in front of me, tilting her head. "Everything okay?"

"Yeah," I said, managing a grin. "Let's ride, little rockstar."

As I mounted my bike and waited for her to climb on, I couldn't shake the nagging feeling that this ride wasn't going to end as smoothly as it started.

After we returned to the Clubhouse, my heart raced with anticipation. The sweet butts had set up a spread of subs, salads, and beans, but my focus was solely on Fuse. We ate and talked, getting to know each other more intimately with each passing moment.

There was something about Fuse that drew me to him. I couldn't resist his charm, his rugged good looks, and the hot attraction that burned me alive. It was as if we were destined to be together, two halves of a whole.

So, when he invited himself into my room later that night, I didn't protest. I quickly showered and threw on an oversized t-shirt before there was a knock on my door. Without hesitation, I let Fuse in. His muscular frame was only covered by sweatpants, no shirt or shoes in sight. I couldn't help but admire his toned physique and the intricate tattoos that adorned his body.

"Ready for round two, little rockstar?" He asked with an intense look in his eyes.

Before I could even respond, he had already taken off my shirt and was examining my body. Insecurities crept into my mind about my small chest, but the way Fuse's eyes roamed over me made all those doubts disappear.

"You are so damn sexy," he growled, picking me up effortlessly and tossing me onto the bed. He quickly discarded his sweatpants and climbed on top of me.

"I've been craving the taste of your pussy since the first time I saw you," he confessed, before diving between my legs. My hips arched involuntarily as he spread me open and began devouring me. His fingers joined in on the action, filling me up as his tongue worked its magic on my sensitive clit.

"You taste incredible," he moaned against me before adding another finger inside of me. The sensations were overwhelming, and before I knew it, I was climaxing hard, screaming his name.

But Fuse wasn't done with me yet. He flipped me over onto my hands and knees and quickly rolled on a condom. I could feel the head of his cock pressing against my entrance before he thrust himself deep inside of me.

"Take it, Shay," he grunted, his hands gripping my breasts firmly as he pounded into me with an intense rhythm. Every thrust sent shockwaves through my body, building up to another orgasm.

"Yes, God, yes!" I cried out as Fuse used his hand to rub my clit, pushing me over the edge once again. My body spasmed uncontrollably as waves of pleasure washed over me. Fuse continued to thrust into me, chasing his own orgasm.

"Fucking hell, this feels good," Fuse growled, throwing his head back and bellowing his release, slowly thrusting, pumping himself dry. Then, getting rid of the condom, falling to the side, he pulled my back against his front; we laid like that for what seemed like hours but, in reality, was probably minutes.

As we lay there, panting and sweating, I couldn't deny the intensity of our connection. And as much as I tried to resist, I knew this was just the beginning of a wild ride with Fuse by my side.

His arm was draped over my waist, his breath warm and even against the nape of my neck. I could feel his heart beating rhythmically against my back, a comforting assurance that he was mine, if only for the moment. There was a deep sigh behind me, resonating with contentment.

"I hope you're not regretting this," Fuse murmured, his voice sounding slightly forlorn. I turned in his arms to face him, our eyes meeting in the dimly lit room.

"Why would I regret anything?" I asked, placing a reassuring hand on his chest. His skin was still warm from our exertions.

Fuse's eyes were searching mine, as though he was trying to read something written within them. "I don't know but I feel like you might," he confessed softly, his thumb tracing idle circles on my hip.

"I don't," I assured him, resting my head on his chest and listening to the steady beat of his heart.

His grip on me tightened slightly as he sighed again. "Good," he said simply. From anyone else it might have sounded curt, or dismissive, but coming from Fuse it was filled with relief and warmth.

Our talks were laced with quiet pauses, comfortable silences where we just lay entwined in each other's arms. The night slowly began to fade into dawn as we drifted in and out of sleep.

When we woke up, I found myself curled up next to him still. His arms were thrown carelessly over me as I laid there, contemplating the man before me. Gently brushing some hair off his face, I took in his features intimately; the stubble on his chin, the slight curve of his lips, his long eyelashes that kissed the top of his cheeks. He was even more mesmerizing when he was sleeping. I traced my fingers over the tattoos peppered across his arm, each one telling a different story.

Just as I was about to doze off again, I felt him stir. His eyes fluttered open to meet mine, a sleepy smile gracing his lips as he pulled me closer. "Hey, rockstar," he murmured against my forehead.

I couldn't help but return his smile, feeling an unexpected warmth blossoming in my chest. "Hey," I whispered back, snuggling deeper into his embrace.

Fuse's hand began to wander down my waist, tracing lazy patterns over my skin that made me shiver in delight. "How about we stay here?" he suggested with a mischievous glint in his eyes.

Laughing softly, I swatted at his wandering hand. "As tempting as that sounds, we've got stuff to do," I reminded him playfully.

He let out a groan of disappointment but didn't release his hold on me. Instead, he opted to shower me with gentle kisses all over my face, causing me to giggle uncontrollably.

Despite the initial plan, we didn't move from that spot until well into the afternoon. We stayed wrapped up in each other's arms, exchanging soft words and gentle touches as time passed us by.

It was then that I realized that maybe this thing between Fuse and me wasn't just a fling. It was something worth taking a chance on.

10

Walking into the basement, I saw Shadow, Vampire, Stonewall, and Viking leaning against the wall. I walked up to them, asking, "I take it we caught our prey?"

"That we did. We had to shoot one of the motherfuckers in the leg. They weren't easy to take down. Fucker tried to bite me," Viking said, scowling.

"Shit, man, I wish I could have seen that. I bet that shit was funny as hell," I laughed at Viking, knowing it would piss him off, and sure enough, his face turned red, scowling even more.

"That's enough, Fuse; we have shit to do right now; Viking can kick your skinny ass later," Shadow said.

About that time, Kickstand, Moreno, and King showed up. Shadow continued, "The men have been separated. Viking, you, Kickstand, Moreno, and King will go into one room. Vampire, Stonewall, and Fuse your with me. Do whatever you need to do to get information. Don't kill until you have it."

With that, we separated into two rooms.

The man was chained to the wall, arms above his head. He had already pissed himself. Our club had a reputation, and he knew he wasn't getting out alive. He just prayed for a quick death as Shadow walked up to him.

"How's our stalker doing tonight? Are you comfortable? Need anything?" Shadow smirked at him. The man said nothing, just looked down at the floor. Shadow grabbed the man's face, making him look at us, saying, "Don't be rude, I'm talking to you, and I want to know some things, and you're going to tell me."

"I ain't telling you shit. You can go ahead and kill me."

Vampire stepped up; he was antsy, brother liked to torture; I think it turned him on or some shit. "Oh, we won't kill you, but you will wish you were dead when we're through with you. Of that, you can be sure."

Looking at Shadow, the man said, "Wait until they get that pretty bitch of yours. She'll be fucked in each hole by so many men. She'll slit her own throat just to have it end."

The man was goading Shadow to kill him, and it might work.

Shadow backhanded him, going for his neck before Stonewall pulled Shadow back. "Don't do it, brother, that's what he wants, for you to kill him. Let Vampire have a go at him."

Vampire pulled out the special knife he used for this stuff and went to work. Within minutes, the man was screaming in agony. This went on for an hour, and the man still wouldn't talk. He finally passed out. He was a tough one.

"We'll stop for a few hours. Hopefully, Viking had better luck. Vampire and I will come back later and continue. I know you two have work in the morning," Shadow said, looking at Stonewall and me.

Vampire knocked on the other door, and Kickstand came out. "So far, all we've gotten out of him is that the men were sent to spy on us, which we already knew. I don't think it'll be long before he cracks."

"Same with us; we're taking a break since our guy passed out. Vampire and I are coming back down in a few hours. Tell Viking to take a break. Sometimes giving them time to think about their situation helps," Shadow said, and Kickstand went back into the room.

"Keep me informed about what's happening; I suppose I'll head back up if you don't need me." I wanted to get back to Shay.

"Will do. We'll have a special meeting to discuss what we find out," Shadow said.

"I'm heading out back for a smoke. I'll be back here in two hours, Shadow," Vampire took off toward the stairs.

Yep, Vampire needed a smoke after torturing the man; it was like sex for him. I didn't get it but to each their own.

I followed Vampire up the stairs, with Shadow right behind me. Both of us are heading back to our women.

I lay in bed, thinking about what I had done. I had broken a major rule and slept with Fuse. Not only did I sleep with Fuse, but I also slept with him after only a few days.

Unheard of for me

And did I *really* want it to go further?

The club lifestyle is not something I've ever wanted. I don't know if any relationship could ever survive it. But Fuse liked women, and I don't see him giving up his ways. No biker I had ever known did. The money, the danger, sweet butts, and easy sex were just too much of a draw to keep these men in a committed relationship.

I am so confused right now. The sex was fantastic. I had never had sex so fast and raw as earlier with Fuse. And damn it, I was looking forward to more of it.

Way more.

I must have fallen asleep at some point because I woke up to Fuse sucking on my nipples with his fingers inside me. I grabbed him by his hair, urging him on and spreading my legs wider and rotating my hips.

"Your pussy is so tight; I can feel it gripping my fingers," Fuse breathed against my breasts.

He shoved in another finger, his fingers teasing my pussy. I was so close to an orgasm when he pulled out his fingers and hovered above me. I could feel his cock, heavy and long, against my inner thigh.

"Look at me," He rasped, his lips finding mine, letting his tongue slide into my mouth to play. His amber eyes locked with mine.

Still holding eye contact, he ripped open a condom he had in reach. Rolling it on, he spread my thighs, sinking every inch of his hard cock into my wet pussy.

"Fuuuuck!" He groaned. "You feel so fucking good, your tight little pussy clenching around my cock." He started to thrust into me, holding himself with his elbows, his eyes bouncing from where we were joined and back to my eyes.

His cock felt so good, and I wanted him to fuck me hard and fast.

And he didn't disappoint.

"Oh God, Fuse, please don't stop," I moaned, my hips thrusting up to meet him thrust for thrust. He changed his angle, turning my moans into screams. "Fuck Fuse, I'm so close. Don't stop, don't stop," I breathlessly chanted.

"Cum, little rockstar, cum all over my cock, milk it dry," He groaned as he fucked me faster, his hips picking up speed. Pumping hard and fast and leaning down, taking my lips as I moaned and shuddered with my orgasm underneath him. His eyes never left mine.

"Fuck Shay," I felt his body stiffen, and with a loud moan, he came, my pussy clenching around his cock with his release.

He pulled out, ridding himself of the condom. He kissed me

gently, pushing my damp hair back from my face, rolling to my side. Both of us are trying to get control of our breathing.

"You drive me crazy, Shay. I came in here wanting to take my time with you, and I lose control and have to be inside you. I can't take it slow and easy."

"It felt so good; I'm not complaining, Fuse; I might have trouble walking tomorrow, but it's worth it," I teased him. But, damn, it was so worth it.

"Call me Scott, little rockstar; I want to hear my name on your lips."

I wasn't going to overthink what that meant. "Okay, Scott, I'll do that; I like it better than Fuse, anyway." I turned in his arms, so my front was to his, and laid my head on his chest. I was asleep within minutes.

11

As I was riding my bike to the garage this morning, my mind went back to last night and waking up to Shay, her lips wrapped around my cock, followed by her riding me so hard I thought I would die with pleasure. Her tattoo ended at her belly button with a dragonfly that looked like it had landed there. When she moved on my cock, it looked like it could fly.

What the fuck was happening to me? I couldn't get enough of her.

I never stayed the night with a woman ever. They never got a chance by me, never bringing them back to my room. I fucked, and I left. That's how I usually roll. No woman ever lived in my head afterward.

Shay did.

Not only was fucking the best I've ever experienced, and that's saying a lot for me, I have been with tons of bitches. But, I also like spending time with her, being close to her. I like her for more than a fuck.

When we parted this morning, all I could think about was getting back to her this evening. And that scared me, but I was helpless to stop it.

Pulling into the garage, I forced my mind to do all the things needed doing today. The sooner I got everything done, the sooner I could leave. Two other brothers worked here with me, Poison and Yankee. Between us, we should finish up early.

As I walked around the front, I saw Lexi standing beside her car.

What the fuck?

"Hey Fuse, my car is making a ticking noise, and I thought you could look at it," Lexi said, thrusting her overflowing tits out and licking her lips.

With narrowed eyes, I looked at her. Things that I used to consider playful when Lexi did them now irritated me. And I knew what she was doing, and it wasn't going to work. For whatever reason, I only wanted Shay, and I didn't want to screw it up.

"What's the real reason you're here, Lexi? I know it's not your car," I snapped.

"I just miss you, Fuse. Since that bitch came around, you don't play anymore," Lexi whined, looking up through her lashes.

"I didn't know it was any of your business what I did, Lexi. And don't call Shay a bitch; it pisses me off. I already told you, if I want your attention, you'll know it and until then, back off."

"So, she *is* just temporary?"

"I didn't fucking say that and you're putting words in my mouth. Now, if you don't need anything, I have work to get done," I said, glaring at Lexi. I'd had enough of this conversation.

"I'm sorry, Fuse, but you always treated me best out of all the guys. I miss being with you. I miss fucking you and I know you miss it too. But if I have to wait for you to get tired of her, I will, and you know where to find me."

She gave me one last hopeful look before turning and getting in her car, driving away.

Lexi is wrong, and I don't miss fucking her. I don't even remember what it felt like to fuck Lexi. And judging by this conversation, I will never touch her again, no matter what happens. She has overstepped in a big way.

Fuck this shit, I have work to do and the sooner I finish, the sooner I get to see my little rockstar.

FUSE

Driving up to the clubhouse, the sound of an acoustic guitar reached me before I even turned the corner. *That's not her electric guitar.* I slowed my steps and spotted Shay sitting out back, her head down, focused on the strings, her fingers plucking out something familiar—*Simple Man* by Lynyrd Skynyrd. The sight of her, so lost in the music, made me stop in my tracks.

Shit. She was beautiful like this. Calm. Untouchable.

An idea struck me, and before I could second-guess it, I jogged upstairs to my room. Digging through my closet, I pulled out an old acoustic guitar. It wasn't much—something I'd picked up when I was sixteen and taught myself to play—but it would do. I dusted it off, tested the strings, and headed back outside.

Shay didn't hear me come up behind her. She was too caught up in the music, eyes closed, swaying gently as she played. Her voice carried softly, full of emotion, and I let myself enjoy it for a moment. Then I strummed the first chords of *Simple Man* right along with her.

Shay turned, her eyes wide with surprise. "Scott, you play?" Her voice was breathless, and the look on her face made me grin. "Why didn't you tell me?"

I shrugged, dropping down onto the bench beside her. "I do play — just not nearly as well as you. It's more of a hobby, something I picked up when I was sixteen to kill time. Never really stuck with it. But when I saw you sitting here with a classical guitar, I figured I'd dust off my skills and join in."

The truth was, I hadn't played in years. No one really knew I could. I wasn't great, but the way Shay's face lit up like I'd pulled some magic trick out of my back pocket? Hell, I'd play every damn day if it got that reaction from her.

"Well then," she said, turning those bow-shaped lips into a teasing smile. "Play with me, Scott."

That smile, paired with the playful wink she threw my way, hit me right in the chest.

So I played.

We spent the next hour trading chords and songs. Shay put me to shame with her talent, her fingers dancing effortlessly across the strings, but I didn't care. For once, I let myself enjoy the moment. Just us, the music, and the warm afternoon sun filtering through the trees.

I couldn't help but wish we had more time. That I could grab her hand, take her upstairs, and spend the rest of the day tangled up in her. But, as always, club business had to come first.

I sighed, setting my guitar aside. "I hate to end this, Shay, but Shadow called Church for six, and I need to get moving."

She stood, slipping her arms around my middle, pressing her cheek lightly against my chest. That simple gesture almost did me in.

"Will I see you later, Scott?" she asked softly, looking up at me with those clear blue eyes.

I smiled, brushing a strand of hair back from her face. "Little rockstar, do you even have to ask? Get something to eat and rest. You're gonna need the energy for later." I sealed the promise with a slow, thorough kiss, lingering just long enough to feel her melt into me. Pulling back, I smacked her playfully on the ass, earning a glare that didn't quite reach her eyes.

I watched her walk away, shaking my head.

Calm the hell down, Fuse. You'll get yours later.

Inside the meeting room, I was the last one to take my seat. Shadow was already standing at the head of the table, his face tight. Whatever he was about to say, I knew it wasn't good.

"After spending the night with our visitors in the basement, we've got some information," Shadow began, his voice hard as he rubbed his temples. "Is it useful? I don't know. Only one man talked. The other didn't make it through the night."

"What did you learn?" I asked, leaning forward.

"The guy Viking worked over said The Fire Dragons paid them to watch us," Shadow explained. "They were gathering intel—patterns, weaknesses, anything they could use against us."

"Exactly what we thought," Soldier said, his tone bitter.

Viking stroked his mustache thoughtfully, a sure sign he wasn't buying it. "Yeah, but he also said Cross wasn't ready to make a move yet. I don't know if I believe that."

"I don't either," Vampire chimed in. "By the time Viking was done with him, he'd say anything to make it stop."

Shadow nodded, his face grim. "Agreed. I think Cross is more than ready. Hell, he's probably been watching us for longer than we realize. We've also got another problem—someone in the club is feeding them information."

The room went silent. I could feel the tension thickening, brothers shifting uncomfortably in their seats.

"Any idea who?" I asked.

Kickstand pulled a folder out and flipped it open. "If I had to put money on it, it's Tommy—the prospect. He's been hanging around for nearly two years, brought in by Barnes before he died. He's dragging his feet on patching in, and honestly, he doesn't seem committed. He's got 'rat' written all over him."

Shadow's gaze narrowed. "We'll keep him under watch. Moreno, you up for tailing him?"

Moreno nodded immediately. "Yeah, I'll handle it. If Tommy's our guy, we'll know soon enough."

Shadow's phone buzzed, and he glanced down. "I've got a run to

West Virginia on Friday to meet with Patch and exchange intel. I've got other business there too. Fuse, you and Lord are coming with me."

I frowned. "Why can't we leave earlier and come back the same day?"

Shadow smirked like he'd been expecting that. "Because I've got a meeting with the contractor building my house in the morning. Shay'll survive a night without you."

"Yeah, Fuse," Vampire added with a laugh. "It's not like you won't have *companionship* at Patch's clubhouse."

"Fuck off, Vampire," I muttered, shaking my head. "I just don't like the idea of us being gone with everything going on."

"I've got a man on each of the women," Shadow said firmly. "Viking will keep an eye on Shay."

I grumbled but knew better than to argue. Club business came first. Always.

"Fine. I'll be ready," I said, though I didn't like it one bit.

Shadow wrapped up the meeting with a warning: "We'll reconvene Sunday unless something changes. Stay sharp."

Viking clapped me on the shoulder as the others started to file out. "I'll keep Shay safe, brother. No worries."

"Thanks, man," I said quietly. "I just don't want her getting caught up in this shit."

Viking nodded. "I got you."

Once the meeting ended, I checked my watch—almost eight. *Shay*. I had no doubt she was in the bar area, so I headed that way, already looking forward to seeing her again.

12

I walked up to the bar and ordered a whiskey sour, letting the cool glass settle in my hand before turning around. That's when I spotted Mary, Lettie, and Joe sitting at a table in the corner, their heads together like they were already plotting something.

Here we go.

I made my way over, plopping down in the empty seat with a sigh.

"Hey, Shay. How's it going, girl?" Lettie greeted me, biting back a sly smile. I knew exactly where this was headed.

"Yeah, Shay. What's up? And not just Fuse's dick," Joe added with a giggle and a wink.

I rolled my eyes, smirking despite myself. "You two are nosey bitches, you know that, right?"

Lettie shrugged. "Is there any other way for a bitch to be? Now fess up—how was it? Fuse walks around here like his dick's gold, and he's been handing it out to you for free. Spill."

Mary, ever the peacekeeper, tried to step in. "Come on, ladies. Maybe she doesn't want to talk about it. It's personal."

"Bullshit." Joe clapped her hands, clearly not backing down. "You don't have to give us the play-by-play. Just give us something. I've watched Fuse strut around here for years, swinging that cock of his like a damn flag. I want the lowdown."

"How do you know we even went there?" I shot back, sipping my drink for effect. "Maybe we haven't gotten that far yet."

Lettie rolled her eyes, like I'd just said something ridiculous. "Please. We're not blind, Shay. The man's been stuck to you since you got here. You'd have to be blind not to see the way he looks at you."

Mary nodded, her tone calm but honest. "They're right. Since I've been here, I've never seen Fuse act this way. Before you, he flirted with everything that had legs. Now? He doesn't look at anyone but you."

The three of them stared me down like interrogators ready to pounce. They were relentless, and I knew I'd have to throw them a bone. That didn't mean I liked hearing about Scott's past—or how much of a man-whore he'd apparently been. All that "swinging his dick around" shit wasn't exactly a confidence booster.

"Fine." I set my drink down, lifting my hand to mime zipping my lips. "Let's just say Scott's got a reason to strut, and that's all you're getting from me."

"Scott?" Joe blinked, clearly surprised. "Is that his name? I'll be damned. I never knew."

"Wow, Shay." Lettie smirked, leaning back in her chair like she'd won a prize. "He must have it bad for you if you've got him telling you his real name. I never thought I'd see Fuse settle down."

I shook my head. "Listen, I don't know what this is between Scott and me. I'm taking it one day at a time. He's a biker, and they're not exactly known for commitment."

Mary tilted her head, giving me that sweet, serene look she always wore. "Sure, they are—when they find the right woman. Shadow's committed to me, and he doesn't screw around. None of the guys do, not when they're serious."

I sighed. "Maybe for some, but I grew up with a different perspective. My dad lived the club life. I saw a lot of shit, and I don't want that for myself." I straightened, determined to change the subject. "Speaking of which, Mary, why do you have a bandage on your shoulder?"

Mary's face brightened, and she pulled the bandage off carefully. "I got a tattoo today—Shadow's mark. It covers the scar where I was shot."

I leaned closer, studying the design. "That's gorgeous." I couldn't hide my admiration. "I've never seen anything like that."

The tattoo was stunning—delicate yet bold. A pink cat curled within blue shadows, and if you looked closely, Shadow's name swirled into the design like smoke. It was creative as hell.

"Lenny—Stonewall—designed it and did the tattoo," Mary said, smiling proudly. "I never knew he had that kind of talent, but I love it. I wasn't sure at first, but I'm glad I did it."

"He's gifted." I sat back, already thinking. "I may have to see what he can design for me. I've been looking for something new."

"Oh, look who just walked in," Lettie said, a teasing lilt to her voice. "And sure as shit, he's looking for Shay." She smirked knowingly. "Here he comes."

I turned, and my stomach did a little flip when I saw Scott heading our way. He cut through the room like he owned the place, his amber eyes locked on me. My heart sped up in response, the way it always seemed to around him.

"Look at all the beauty at this one table," Scott said with a whistle, a wicked grin spreading across his face. "Enough to make a man weep."

"Give it a rest, Fuse." Lettie rolled her eyes, standing up. "There's only one beauty you're interested in at this table, and we'll leave you two alone. Come on, ladies."

Mary and Joe followed, each giving me a wink and a smirk as they walked off. I shot them a glare, but it didn't matter—they were already laughing.

Scott didn't waste any time. He pulled me up against him, his hands warm against my waist as he whispered, "They're right, you know. My interest is for you only, Shay."

My pulse quickened, my breath catching. I looked up at him, searching his face, and the intensity in his eyes nearly undid me. "Well then," I said, my voice coming out huskier than I intended, "maybe we need to explore that."

Grabbing his hand, I led him toward the stairs, my heart pounding harder with every step. I didn't care who saw us or what they thought. Right now, it was just Scott and me.

And that night, we didn't leave his room until morning.

13

The next few days blurred into a routine I couldn't get enough of. I'd spend the night with Shay, head to work, then haul my ass back to the clubhouse to spend the evening with her again. It was like my whole life had started revolving around her.

And fuck if it didn't scare the shit out of me.

I couldn't keep my hands off her—couldn't get enough of the way she smiled at me like I wasn't just another biker to her. Being with her felt different from anything I'd ever known. It wasn't just the physical pull, though *that* was intense enough to drive me crazy. It was the way she got under my skin. The way she was in my head even when she wasn't around.

Now, riding toward the West Virginia clubhouse, the steady thrum of my bike beneath me, those thoughts twisted tighter. My past had a way of sneaking up on me—clawing its way into my brain, spreading doubt like a disease.

What if I let Shay in completely, and she leaves me?

Every other woman in my life had walked away. My mom. My sister. Even the first girl I thought I cared about, back when I was stupid enough to believe in love. They'd all left me with nothing but empty promises and a bad taste in my mouth. I'd learned to live without trust—to take what I wanted without giving anything real in return.

But Shay? She was different.

The thought of not seeing her tonight was already gnawing at me, and that scared me even more. I missed her, and it had only been a few hours. What the hell was wrong with me? Since when did I become *that* guy?

And what if I couldn't be the man she needed? Could I really be faithful to one woman? I'd never wanted to before. Hell, I didn't even know if I was capable of it. But for Shay... *I somehow knew I could.*

"Fuck," I muttered under my breath, gripping the throttle a little harder.

The wind whipped around me as we rolled up to the West Virginia clubhouse, the sound of bikes cutting through the early evening. This place was different from ours. The energy here was wild and unrestrained, like a barely contained storm waiting to explode.

We parked our bikes, the engines rumbling to silence one by one, and I swung my leg off mine. Even from the outside, the party was in full swing—music blasting, laughter carrying through the open doors, and the smell of smoke and whiskey hanging in the air.

Shadow climbed off his bike and pulled off his gloves. His face was as unreadable as ever, but I could see the tension in his shoulders. There was business to handle tonight, and Shadow never fucked around when it came to that.

"I've got shit to talk to Patch about," he said, already heading for the clubhouse doors. "I'll be in his office for the next few hours."

I nodded as he disappeared inside, my eyes scanning the scene around me. West Virginia's clubhouse was a lot rowdier than ours— no restrictions on when or where the party could happen. Women leaned against bikes, hanging on club brothers like they didn't have a care in the world. The music was loud, the crowd already buzzed, and the wild energy pulsed like a living thing.

Normally, this kind of scene would've pulled me right in. I'd grab a drink, flirt with whoever was closest, and lose myself in the party. But not tonight. My mind was still with Shay, even here. I could see her in my head—sitting with her guitar, her fingers flying across the strings, or shooting me that sass-filled smirk that drove me insane.

The thought brought a half-smile to my face.

Goddamn, Fuse. You're gone.

"Yo, Fuse!" Lord's voice pulled me back. He was grinning, a beer already in hand. "You gonna stand there all night, or are you gonna join the fun?"

"Yeah, yeah," I said, forcing a smirk as I followed him toward the bar.

But as I grabbed a beer and looked around, all I could think about was getting back to Shay. It was like no matter where I went or what I did, she was there in the back of my mind. And the longer this went on, the more I knew one thing for sure.

This wasn't just a fling.

This was dangerous.

It was still early, so things were just getting started. I sat down with Lord and started drinking, and I knew I shouldn't now with my mind running me in circles. Drugs were flowing all around us. I wasn't into hard drugs. I did smoke pot, so I accepted the joint Lord handed me.

After a bit, we moved to a couch in the corner. I was drunk and high and I should have been enjoying the party, but Shay kept my mind busy. I couldn't stop thinking about her. Then, two bitches came up in front of Lord and me and started dancing. I knew I should get up and leave, but my mind wanted to know: could I refuse sex with these women? Be faithful to Shay. I thought it would be a good idea to test the theory in my drunken state.

I'm a stupid fuck.

Their clothes started coming off. The bitch in front of me had huge tits, and I would have jumped on her at one time. But she looked all wrong. She was too overblown, just too much—not my little rockstar.

The woman was sitting on my lap, grinding against my cock, shoving those enormous globes in my face. I didn't even touch her with my hands. I couldn't.

She went for the button on my jeans, undoing it. I stopped her, shoving her off me. This was all wrong, and I stood up. "Sorry, babe, I need some air."

I walked outside, breathing hard to the point of being sick. I almost fucked up. Could I have fucked her with enough alcohol and grinding on my dick? Who the fuck knows, but I didn't want to find out.

A casual fuck didn't appeal to me, and that's all it would have been. Shay was different from other women.

Was it love?

Fuck if I know. I only know what I feel.

And Shay was all I wanted.

I answered the phone with a smirk. "Hey, little rockstar, I thought you had a show."

Hearing her voice immediately calmed the storm raging in my chest. Just looking into those baby-blue eyes always grounded me, but tonight, I didn't have that luxury.

"I do. We're taking a break," Shay said, her tone edged with concern. "I was worried when I didn't hear from you. I called before the show, but you didn't answer."

Her voice was soft, but I could hear the suspicion creeping into it. *Shit.* I ran a hand through my hair, feeling cornered.

"Sorry," I said, trying to sound casual. "It's so loud in there; I must have missed it. By the time we got here, it was almost time for your show, so I figured I'd wait until after to call."

It was a lie—one that felt like a weight in my gut. I hated lying to Shay. The truth was, I hadn't called because my head was too fucked up, and now I was paying for it.

She narrowed her eyes through the phone, and her voice dropped an octave. "Are you drunk, Scott?"

I opened my mouth, trying to come up with something—*anything*—that didn't sound like bullshit. But before I could speak, I felt a pair of arms snake around me from behind. A sultry voice purred against my ear, "Hey, Fuse. Come back inside so we can finish what we started."

Fuuuck. My stomach dropped. I pulled away from the woman like she was on fire, spinning around to glare at her. I didn't even know her fucking name, but she wore a smug grin, probably thinking she was in for another round.

My phone buzzed in my hand. I glanced at it and cursed under my breath. Shay had hung up.

"SHIT! SHIT! SHIT!" I roared, kicking the side of the wall, sending the bitch in front of me scrambling away.

I raked a hand through my hair, pacing as anger and panic rose inside me.

How the fuck did I let this happen?

"Calm the fuck down, Fuse. What's your problem?" Shadow's voice cut through the noise I was making. He and Patch had walked up, both of them staring at me like I'd lost my damn mind.

"I was on the phone with Shay when this bitch walked up behind me, saying shit," I ground out, throwing a glare at the woman who couldn't seem to get lost, still lingering a few feet away. "Shay didn't even give me a chance to explain. She thinks I cheated."

Shadow raised an eyebrow, his expression unreadable. "Let me give you a little wisdom when it comes to women." He leaned back against the wall, crossing his arms. "I came through the bar on my way out here. You had a bitch grinding on your lap, rubbing her tits in your face. To a woman like Shay, that's cheating. Doesn't matter if you didn't want her. Doesn't matter if you came to your senses and walked away. *She knows you went there.* That's all that counts."

"Fuck, Shadow." I clenched my fists, frustration boiling over. "I didn't even want her! I was testing myself, all right? Letting my old insecurities get the best of me. And now I've fucked everything up." I paused, my voice dropping as the reality of the situation hit me. "I know Shay. She won't forgive this."

Patch snorted, shaking his head. "Shadow's right, man. Women don't take shit like that lightly. That's why I don't have an ol' lady—too damn complicated." He turned and walked off, leaving me alone with Shadow.

I looked at him helplessly. "How do you do it, Shadow? Keep so in control. Not let the fears take hold?"

Shadow gave me a long, measured look before answering. "For starters, I don't put myself in the situation you did tonight. Notice I wasn't in the middle of that mess inside. It's not because those women don't tempt me—*they don't*. But I don't want to send mixed signals to Mary. She's too important to me." He paused, his gaze hardening. "I feel the fear, Fuse. Every damn day. I think about what would happen if I lost her, but I don't let it rule me. I sure as hell don't test myself with random pussy. When the fear gets bad, I get on my bike and ride until my head clears."

I exhaled sharply, staring at the darkened road beyond the clubhouse. "I need to ride back tonight. I have to talk to her—make her understand." My voice was raw with desperation. "I don't know how, but in the short time I've known Shay, she's become... important to me."

Shadow's expression softened just slightly, because he knew exactly what I meant. "That's how it happens," he said quietly. "When it's the right woman, it hits you fast. As soon as you look at her, you just know. But you're not riding back tonight, Fuse. You're too drunk, and even if you weren't, Shay won't talk to you right now. You'll just make it worse."

He was right. I was in no condition to ride, and knowing Shay, she'd hang up on me the second I called again.

"Go sleep it off," Shadow said, his voice firm but not unkind. "Talk to her tomorrow, when you've got a clearer head."

The fight drained out of me, replaced by frustration and guilt. I nodded once, running a hand over my face. "Yeah. Fine."

Turning, I headed back into the clubhouse, my steps heavy. I didn't bother stopping at the bar or talking to anyone. I went straight to my room and slammed the door behind me.

Dropping onto the bed, I stared up at the ceiling, my mind racing. *How the fuck do I fix this?*

Shay's face kept flashing in my mind—the hurt, the suspicion, the way she'd sounded when she asked if I was drunk. I couldn't blame her for hanging up. To her, it looked bad. And maybe Shadow was right—maybe I *had* fallen into my own damn trap.

I'd let my insecurities push me back into old habits. And now? I was paying for it.

Rolling onto my side, I punched my pillow and muttered to

myself, "I'll make this right, Shay. Even if it kills me."

Sleep didn't come easy that night. My thoughts were a chaotic mess of guilt, regret, and the gnawing ache of missing her.

I dropped the phone, the thud of it hitting the floor echoing in the quiet room. My legs gave out, and I slid down until I was sitting with my back against the wall, my knees pulled up to my chest. I buried my face in my hands, fighting back the tears that burned behind my eyes.

How did I let this happen?

I thought we had something real. I *felt* it—something more than just a fling or a casual connection. But that ache in my gut, the one I tried to ignore when Scott didn't call or answer his phone, had been right all along. That's why I did the video call—I needed to see his face. To hear the lie straight from his mouth.

I was such a fool.

This is all my fault.

I knew better than to get involved with a biker. I'd grown up around club life. I knew how it worked—how men like Fuse used women and moved on without a second thought. But Scott... *Goddamn him,* he made me believe he was different.

I let him in. I let myself start to care about him. And now, it felt like he'd ripped the ground right out from under me.

The door creaked open, pulling me out of my spiral. I quickly wiped at my face as Gabe, the band's drummer, stepped into the room. He crouched down in front of me, his expression tight with concern.

"Shay? You okay?"

I forced myself to take a deep breath, pushing the hurt down, locking it up where no one could see. "Yeah," I said, my voice rough. "I'm fine. I just got off the phone. I was about to head out." I grabbed the edge of the wall and lifted myself off the floor. My legs felt like jelly, but I forced them to hold.

Gabe didn't look convinced. "Here," he said, holding something out. "These were outside the door. The card has your name on it."

I blinked at the bouquet of flowers in his hands. Beautiful, fresh blooms—lilies and roses—that would've been stunning if not for the icy dread that slid through me the moment I saw them. My stomach churned as I plucked the card from the arrangement.

Leave town, or the next flowers you receive will be for your grave.

The words stared back at me, sharp as a knife.

"What the hell?" I whispered under my breath. A chill ran down my spine, but anger quickly boiled over the fear.

Was this some kind of sick joke?

Whoever this was, whatever they wanted—they could go straight to hell. I wasn't in the mood for this shit right now. If this was some psycho club girl who wanted Fuse, she could have him. His cheating ass wasn't worth this kind of drama.

With a snarl, I tossed the flowers straight into the trash. "Thanks, Gabe," I muttered, brushing past him. "I'll see you later."

I didn't wait for his response as I headed out to finish the show.

The music had always been my escape, and tonight, I threw everything I had into the final set. By the time I hit the last chord, my chest was heaving, my fingers aching, but my mind was clearer. My hurt had turned to anger, and that anger drove me forward.

Fuse knew how I felt about cheating. He knew what my father put my mom through and what I swore I'd never let happen to me. And he *played* me—made me believe he was different when he wasn't.

Stupid, Shay. You knew better.

Backstage, I packed up my guitar, shoving it into the case with a little more force than necessary. I was snapping the latches closed when I saw Viking headed my way. The guy was a wall of muscle and intimidation, every bit as big and cold as his name implied. His ice-blue eyes seemed to pierce straight through me.

"You heading home, Shay?" His deep voice rumbled, low and steady.

"Yeah." I stood straight, trying to look unbothered. "I'm taking off now. I'm pretty tired tonight." Tired. Depressed. Hollow. But I wasn't going to say that.

Viking gave me a long look, his expression unreadable. "Make sure you go straight to the clubhouse," he said finally. "Check in with someone when you get there."

"Okay, I will."

Without another word, he turned on his heel and walked off, leaving me standing there with a cold chill crawling over my skin. Viking didn't talk much, but when he did, people listened. And the fact that he was telling me to check in had me on edge. Something wasn't right.

I grabbed my guitar case and walked out to my car. The night was quiet, the parking lot half-empty now, but I still glanced over my shoulder as I loaded my gear into the backseat.

Sliding into the driver's seat, I gripped the wheel tightly, tapping down the hurt and the worry swirling inside me. I didn't have the energy to deal with any of it tonight. Right now, I just wanted to get back to the clubhouse, take a long, hot shower, and crawl into bed.

I put the car in drive and pulled out of the lot, the headlights cutting through the darkness as I headed toward the only place that felt even a little bit like home.

But no matter how fast I drove, I couldn't outrun the thoughts chasing me.

Fuse's voice, the way he looked at me, the way he kissed me. All of it haunted me. And yet, that card—the words still burned into my brain—sent shivers through me.

Leave town or the next flowers you receive will be for your grave.

Whoever sent it wasn't playing around and had it bad for Fuse.

You're fucking welcome to him—*whoever* you are.

14

We rolled back into the clubhouse around eleven on Saturday morning. I was stone-cold sober, and the reality of what I'd done hit me square in the gut like a sledgehammer.

How the fuck could I have been so stupid?

Shay would never forgive me—I knew it. She'd told me why she didn't date bikers, why she avoided the life altogether. I'd been the one to prove her right. Just another disappointment. Another reason for her to keep her walls up.

Walking through the clubhouse doors, I looked around, searching for her. The bar area was quiet for once, the usual noise toned down this early in the day.

Shay wasn't there.

I climbed the stairs to her room, my boots heavy against the wood floor, and knocked. Nothing. *Shit.* I stood there for a second, debating whether to wait, but my gut told me she wouldn't be inside.

Back downstairs, I spotted Jane sitting with Silver and Reader at a table in the corner. I made my way over, my voice rough as I asked, "Hey, Jane, have you seen Shay?"

Jane tilted her head, brows furrowing. "Haven't seen her since breakfast."

"She was outside earlier," Reader added, giving me a knowing look. "Playing her guitar."

"Thanks," I muttered, already turning for the back door.

Stepping outside, I spotted her instantly. Shay was sitting alone at one of the old picnic tables, her back to me, the soft melody of her guitar carrying through the air. The way she played—so lost in the music—hit me like a punch to the chest. Her dark hair fell forward, obscuring part of her face, and I couldn't help but take a moment to look at her. She was *so* damn beautiful, it hurt.

How the hell did I almost throw this away?

I moved closer, and the second she realized I was there, her entire body stiffened. She stopped playing, straightening up like she was bracing for a fight. Lifting her chin, she turned to me, and the look in her blue eyes was pure ice.

"Don't bother, Fuse," she sneered, her voice sharp enough to cut. "Growing up, I heard every excuse known to man thrown at my mom. So, save it for someone who gives a shit."

She stood, slinging her guitar over her back and starting to walk away. I couldn't let her leave—not like this. Stepping forward, I grabbed her arm gently, trying to get her to stop.

"Just give me a chance to explain, Shay," I said, my voice low, pleading.

She yanked her arm free like my touch burned her, turning on me with fire in her eyes. "Don't you *touch* me!" she hissed, glaring up at me. "I mean it, Fuse. Forget we ever met."

The venom in her words stung more than I cared to admit. My jaw tightened, but I pushed through it, desperate to get her to hear me out.

"Shay, I messed up," I said, the words coming fast, raw. "But I didn't fuck that bitch. I was just—" I ran a hand through my hair, searching for the right words. "I was confused about things, letting my mind mess with me. I let old insecurities take over, testing myself, but that's on me. I only want you, Shay. Just you."

Her laugh was bitter, her smirk full of something that made my stomach turn.

"Oh, that's a new one," she shot back. "You were just 'testing yourself,' so you went looking for comfort from some random chick. And I'm supposed to what? Applaud you for walking away before you went too far? God, Fuse. You're a *typical* biker." She spat the word like it left a bad taste in her mouth. "Running to sweet butts every time you've got a problem."

Her words hit their mark, sharp and unforgiving, but she wasn't done.

"Lucky for me, I'm not confused," she continued, stepping closer, her tone colder than ever. "You reminded me exactly why I don't want this life. I'm not some desperate biker groupie hoping to be someone's old lady. So go back to your club women, Fuse. They're all yours."

She turned and walked away, her steps steady and sure, leaving me standing there like a goddamn idiot.

Every instinct in my body screamed at me to go after her, to pull her into my arms and make her listen. But I knew it wouldn't do any good. Not right now. She was too pissed off, too hurt to hear a word I had to say.

I watched her walk inside, the door shutting behind her like a final nail in a coffin. My fists clenched at my sides, frustration burning through me. I wanted to fix this, to *fix us*, but how the hell was I supposed to undo the damage I'd done?

I let out a shaky breath, my mind racing.

Give her space.

It was the smart move, but fuck, it went against everything I felt right now. I wanted to drag her back, kiss the anger right out of her, and make her see how much she meant to me.

Instead, I stayed rooted to the spot, staring at the empty doorway.

"I'll fix this, Shay," I muttered under my breath, the promise more to myself than anyone else. "You'll see."

But as much as I wanted to believe it, I couldn't shake the nagging voice in the back of my mind.

What if you already lost her?

I shut the door to my room, leaning my forehead against the wood as I exhaled slowly. My breaths came shaky, like I couldn't quite get enough air.

God, that was harder than I thought.

Facing Fuse—hearing his excuses, *again*—was like twisting a knife deeper into a wound that hadn't even begun to heal. Of course, I knew he'd have something to say. Men *always* do. But what really stung was how much I *wanted* to believe him—that he didn't fuck that woman.

The pain clawing at my chest was unbearable, and the worst part? I had to fight not to show him how much it hurt. I'd rather walk through fire barefoot than let Fuse know how much he meant to me.

Stupid jerk.

I pushed off the door, forcing myself to stand straight. No way in hell was I going to hide up here and give him the satisfaction of thinking I was avoiding him. Straightening my shoulders, I pulled myself together and headed back downstairs.

The bar area was quiet—well, quieter than usual for a Saturday afternoon. A couple of men were playing pool, their laughter sounding under the steady thump of Metallica's *Sad But True*. On one of the worn leather couches, Wrath and Domino lounged with a couple of the sweet butts on their laps.

Lexi was perched on Wrath's knee, looking like a smug little queen, her eyes locking on me the second I walked in. Her smile said *I won, you lost*, and my fists curled at my sides before I forced myself to look away.

Screw her.

I sighed quietly, wishing Mom were here, but I knew she'd gone out with Silver for the afternoon. At least *someone* was having a good day.

Steeling myself, I walked to the bar and slid onto a stool, motioning for the prospect behind the counter. "Vodka Spritz," I said, offering a quick smile.

As I sipped my drink, trying to look casual, Black settled onto the stool next to me, his presence big and impossible to ignore.

"Hey, Shay," he said, flashing that easy smile of his. "Mind if I sit here?"

Thank God for the distraction. At this point, I'd talk to *anyone* just to keep from feeling like a lost puppy. "Nope, not at all."

He leaned closer, resting his forearms on the bar, golden eyes fixed on me in that way these bikers all seemed to perfect. "You know, I'm planning on catching your show later. You're terrific, you know that?"

I couldn't help the small smile that tugged at my lips. "Thanks, Black. I enjoy it. My music keeps me sane." I tilted my head, eyeing him. "Weren't you there last night too?"

"Front and center," he confirmed, grinning. "Like I said, you're good. And I like watching you." He paused, his tone dropping just enough to make me wary. "So... what's up with you and Fuse?"

The mention of Fuse sent my spine straight, but I smoothed my expression, lifting an eyebrow. "Nothing. Why?"

Black tilted his head slightly, a mischievous glint in his eyes. "Because Fuse just walked in, and he looks like he wants to kill me."

My pulse jumped before I could stop it. *Of course* he'd walk in now. And of course, he'd be glaring at me like I'd done something wrong.

Well, screw that.

The devil in me—the one tired of being hurt and humiliated— made me lean in closer to Black. My voice was just loud enough for

Fuse to hear. "Fuse decided our relationship wasn't worth it. So he has no say in what I do now."

Black smirked, playing along. "No shit? I figured he was into you. That's why I backed off." He gave me a slow, lazy grin. "What do you say we have a drink after your set? No strings attached."

I *should* have said no. Black was a flirt, and we both knew this was a game. But I couldn't resist. Out of the corner of my eye, I saw Fuse stalking closer, his anger practically rolling off him in waves.

"Sure," I said, giving Black a sugary smile. "Meet me backstage after the show."

Fuse's voice hit like a clap of thunder. "What the fuck, Shay? Moving on *quickly*, aren't you?"

I turned slowly to face him, tilting my chin up defiantly. "No, Fuse," I said, my voice dripping with venom. "I'm just *testing* myself. You know how that is, right?" I shot him a saccharine smile, adding, "See you tonight, Black."

Before Fuse could get another word out, I slid off the barstool and sauntered away, my heart pounding in my chest.

God, that felt good.

Sure, it was petty. Sure, it might backfire. But for once, I felt like I had the upper hand. Fuse could stew in his jealousy all he wanted. And all it would cost me was one drink with Black.

15

I got to *The Unlimited* early, trailing Shay to make sure she made it okay. She didn't need to know I was watching out for her, and I wasn't exactly proud of myself for acting like a damn stalker. But after her little stunt with Black earlier, my head was all kinds of messed up.

Black.

Just the thought of him sitting there, smiling at her like he had a shot, made my fists clench. After she left, I'd made it clear—*crystal* fucking clear—that Shay was mine. I told him to back off. He hadn't said a word, just looked at me and walked away. For the first time in my life, I'd nearly lost it over a woman. I'd never fought a brother over anyone before, but if Black so much as touched Shay, I'd beat him bloody without a second thought.

Viking walked into the office a few minutes later and dropped into his chair. "Didn't expect to see you here tonight."

"I'm watching Shay play. Missed her set last night." My tone dared him to challenge me on it.

Viking raised a brow, his cold blue gaze sharp. "Last I heard, you had a club whore grinding on your dick at Patch's place. Figured you were done with Shay." He shrugged, like it didn't matter one way or another.

My jaw locked. "Somebody has a big fucking mouth," I ground out. "Yeah, I made a mistake, but I stopped before it went too far. What is this, Viking? Are we gossiping like old ladies now?"

He chuckled, not the least bit phased by my attitude. "Don't get defensive, Fuse. You brought this shit on yourself." He leaned back, folding his arms across his chest. "I don't care who fuck or don't fuck. Just making an observation."

I didn't bother replying. I was done with the conversation.

The bar was already packed when I walked out, but I ignored the crowd and headed straight for the front row. Sure enough, Black was already there. I took the empty seat next to him. He didn't say a word, and I didn't bother starting anything, but I wasn't about to let him make another move.

Finally, the band hit the stage.

The second Shay stepped into the spotlight, the rest of the world fell away. She was something else up there—fierce, confident, so fucking sexy it hurt. Her guitar strap rested across her shoulder, that black instrument gleaming as she shredded through the first song. Every movement of her body, every beat of the music, got under my skin and straight to my cock.

Then she sang *"I Hate Myself for Loving You"* by Joan Jett, her voice dripping with attitude and fire. And yeah, I *knew* the song was directed at me.

Hell, I deserved it.

Black leaned back in his chair, smirking to himself, and I swear my blood pressure spiked. I forced myself to get up and leave before I did something stupid—like punching him in the face.

As I made my way backstage, I heard the sound I dreaded most.

"Fusie! Wait up!"

Shit.

Kim.

But then an idea hit me, and for the first time all night, I grinned. I stopped, turning to her with my most charming smile. "Hey, Kim. I've got a huge favor to ask."

She blinked up at me, her face lighting up like a damn Christmas tree. "Sure, Fusie! You know I'd do *anything* for you."

Perfect.

"See my buddy over there?" I pointed across the room to Black, who was still seated up front, oblivious. "He's having a rough time. His girl left him, and he's been pretty torn up about it. He could use someone to cheer him up—keep him company for a bit, you know?"

Kim's eyes practically sparkled. "Aww, poor guy. You think I can help?"

"Absolutely." I gave her my best *trust me, babe* smile. "He might try to push you away at first, but don't let him. He needs someone to help him move on."

She giggled and flipped her hair. "Don't worry, Fusie. I'll make him feel *all* better."

"Great. And let me know how it goes, yeah?"

"Of course!" she squealed, strutting off in Black's direction like a woman on a mission.

I should've felt guilty about using her like that, but I didn't. All's fair in love and war, and right now, Shay was *worth* the fight.

I slipped backstage and waited.

It wasn't long before I heard the final song wrap up and the sound of boots clattering against the wooden floor. Then Shay walked in, her hair damp with sweat, her guitar case in hand. She froze when she saw me.

Her face hardened, and she turned toward the door.

"Don't," I said, stepping in front of her before she could leave. "We need to talk, Shay."

She lifted her chin, her voice cold as ice. "Fuse, let me go. I'm supposed to meet Black."

"Fuck that. Black's busy." I met her glare head-on. "We need to talk. I need you to understand what happened—and forgive me."

Her cheeks flushed, and I could see her pulse fluttering at her throat. "Fuse, you can't just *force* me to listen to you."

"I can, and I am," I said, softer this time, but no less determined. "I fucked up, Shay. I know that. But you have to understand... this is all new to me. You—what I feel for you—it happened so fast, it scared the shit out of me. I handled it wrong, I know that, but I didn't want her, Shay. I swear to you, I only want you."

She stared at me for a long moment, her expression unreadable. The silence was deafening. I held my breath, waiting—hoping—that I'd said enough.

Before she could speak, I took her lips in mine, pushing my tongue into her mouth. She resisted and then went all in. Her hands went into my hair as our tongues danced together. She was grinding her pussy against my cock. I was ready to lead her to the couch when someone banged on the door. Shay pushed me away, ending our make-out session.

Thinking it was Black, I was surprised when I heard Viking's voice instead.

"Shay, are you in there?"

What the fuck does Viking want with Shay?

I opened the door before Shay could say anything, and she quickly composed herself behind me. Viking stood there, his expression as serious as ever.

"Good, you're here too, Fuse. We've got a problem. Security was making rounds outside and saw someone beating the shit out of your car, Shay."

Shay gasped, her hand flying to her chest. "Why would someone target my car?"

I immediately went to her, pulling her close to calm her down. My blood was already boiling. "Did they see who did it?" My voice came out low and lethal. Someone was about to die.

"No," Viking said grimly. "They took off on foot, and security couldn't catch them. Kickstand's pulling the camera feeds now, so we'll have something soon. Shay, do you have any idea who might want to mess with you? Anyone with a grudge?"

Shay frowned, thinking for a minute before answering. "I didn't think anything of it at the time because I figured it was just a cast-off fling of Fuse..."

My head snapped toward her. "What the fuck, Shay?"

She ignored me, narrowing those icy blue eyes. "...But someone's been leaving me notes. They said I should leave town and stay away from Fuse."

I let her go, pacing in the small space. "You didn't think that was worth mentioning?" I growled, my temper flaring.

Shay shot daggers at me, crossing her arms tightly over her chest. "It's not *my* fault you're a manwhore, Fuse. The first thing I thought was some jealous bitch with a score to settle."

"Enough," Viking said sharply, cutting us both off before I could respond. "Shay, where were these notes left? And do you still have them?"

Shay sighed, the tension easing from her shoulders just a little. "The first one was on my car after we practiced Monday night. The second one showed up with a bouquet of flowers outside my door last night. Gabe found them. I threw both of them away."

Viking stroked his beard, deep in thought. "We'll pull the camera feeds from Monday and Friday. Shay, until we figure out who's behind this, don't go anywhere alone. Fuse, take her back to the clubhouse tonight. I'll keep Kickstand updated."

With that, Viking left, leaving just the two of us. I turned to Shay, my frustration barely held in check.

"You should've said something, Shay. This might be tied to club business, and it could be dangerous."

She snorted and glared at me. "How was I supposed to know that, Fuse? And don't even get me started on last night. You were too busy 'finding yourself' or some shit with another chick to care what was happening to me."

Her words were like a gut punch, but I held my ground. "Shay, for fuck's sake, can we stop bringing up last night? I messed up. I know I did. I can't take it back, but I'll do whatever it takes to make it right. I get that it'll take time for you to trust me again, but can we at least try?"

Shay shook her head, hurt flashing in her eyes before she quickly masked it. "No, Fuse. What's the next excuse going to be? And the one after that? You had my trust, and you broke it the first chance you got."

I sighed heavily, running a hand through my hair. This was going to be harder than I thought, but I wasn't walking away. Shay wasn't just another girl, and I wasn't going to let this be the end. I'd fucked up, but I wasn't done fighting for her.

"Fine," I said finally, softening my tone. "I'll let it go for now. Get ready, and we'll check out the damage to your car. Then I'm taking you back to the clubhouse."

"I can find my own ride back, Fuse. I'm sure Black is still around," she muttered, like she was trying to provoke me.

My fists clenched at the mention of his name. "Just get ready, Shay. I'm taking you back. If Black hasn't shown up by now, he's not going to."

She huffed, clearly pissed but resigned to losing this battle. "Fine," she grumbled. "I'll leave my guitar here since I can't exactly take it on your bike."

As she headed to pack up, I stayed rooted to the spot, watching her.

She's worth it, I reminded myself again.

Even if I had to fight her every step of the way, Shay was worth it.

I followed Fuse out of the club, my footsteps heavy with dread. As we approached my car, my stomach dropped. The destruction was worse than I'd imagined. My poor Corolla was unrecognizable—windows shattered, tires slashed, and dents covering every inch, as if someone had gone to town on it with a baseball bat.

I froze, my chest tightening as tears threatened to fall. "Why?" I whispered, more to myself than anyone.

Why would someone do this to me?

Fuse let out a low curse under his breath. "Shit, Shay. I don't think there's any salvaging it. I'll have the rollback come get it in the morning."

I clenched my fists, trying to fight off the overwhelming frustration. "This fucking sucks. I can't afford another car, Fuse. I only have liability on it. I'm so screwed." My voice cracked, and I groaned, wiping at my eyes angrily.

"Hey," Fuse said softly, stepping closer. "We'll figure something out, okay? For now, let's get out of here. Whoever did this might still be lurking."

I barely registered the way he took my arm, steering me gently toward his bike. I was too numb to argue, too overwhelmed to care that Fuse was Fuse. My thoughts swirled like a storm—anger, hurt, and confusion all tangled together.

He handed me a helmet, and I climbed onto the back of his bike without a word. As I settled behind him, I realized how comforting his presence felt—strong, solid, steady. *Don't think about that, Shay*, I scolded myself. I wrapped my arms around him, holding on tighter than I probably needed to.

The roar of the engine and the hum of the bike beneath me pulled me out of my spiral. I pressed my face against Fuse's back, letting the vibrations calm me, the wind brushing away some of the weight on my shoulders.

By the time we pulled into the clubhouse parking lot, I felt steadier—just enough to fake it until I could be alone. I slid off the bike, handing him the helmet.

"Thanks for the ride, Fuse," I mumbled over my shoulder as I turned to walk inside.

He looked like he wanted to say something, but instead, he just shook his head, pocketed the helmet, and rode off toward the garage.

Inside, the bar area was alive with the usual activity of a

Saturday night. The music was loud, the men rowdy, and the club girls draped themselves over whoever would let them. It was like a keg party from high school, but somehow worse. I ignored it all and scanned the room until I spotted my mom sitting at the bar with Silver.

The moment Mom saw me, her expression changed. "What's the matter, sweetie?" She stood up, concern written all over her face.

"Somebody trashed my car, Mom," I said, my voice breaking as I threw myself into her arms. "I don't know why or who, but it happened while I was playing the show. My car is completely ruined."

"Oh, Shay." She rubbed my back soothingly. "It'll be okay, baby. The important thing is that you're safe. I'm just glad whoever did it took their frustrations out on the car instead of you."

Silver stood, his towering frame adding weight to his words. "Does Shadow know about this?"

"Viking does," I replied, wiping at my eyes. "I'm sure he'll tell him. Kickstand is already going through the security footage."

Silver's expression darkened. "Listen to me, Shay. Don't go anywhere alone, you hear me? Take one of the men with you, even if you think it's nothing. This isn't a joke."

"I won't," I promised weakly. "Not like I have a car to go anywhere now anyway." I tried to sound casual, but I could see the worry deepen on Mom's face. I hated that.

Before she could say anything else, the front door opened, and Fuse walked in.

And just like clockwork, Lexi was all over him, her arms snaking around him like she couldn't get close enough.

I froze, my entire body tensing as I watched him push her away, visibly annoyed. But it didn't matter. That was the straw that broke the camel's back.

Enough.

I turned and bolted from the room, tears I couldn't hold back anymore spilling down my cheeks.

By the time I made it upstairs and into my room, I felt humiliated and furious at myself. I slammed the door, locking it behind me before sinking onto the bed. I buried my face in the pillow, letting the sobs come.

A knock at the door startled me, followed by Fuse's voice. "Shay, let me in. Please, I just want to talk."

I stayed silent, my breathing shaky. I couldn't talk to him right now. I couldn't let him see me like this, broken and vulnerable. After a few long moments, I heard his footsteps retreat down the hall.

Mom texted me soon after to check on me. I knew she understood that I needed space. She always did.

Exhausted and drained, I grabbed some pajamas, changed quickly, and crawled into bed. The room felt too big and empty, and the image of my ruined car mixed with Lexi's smug face played over and over in my head. I curled up under the blankets, letting my anger turn to sadness as I drifted into an uneasy sleep.

Walking down the hall from Shay's room, I spotted Lexi waiting for me like a vulture circling its prey. My anger spiked the second I saw her smug expression. "What the fuck do you want?" I hissed, my voice low and dangerous.

She flinched, taking a small step back, but quickly plastered on a nervous smile. "I'm sorry, Fuse. I didn't know you and Shay were still a thing. Word around here was you were with someone else last night. I wouldn't have done that if I'd known..."

"Cut the shit, Lexi." I shot her a glare that could peel paint off a wall. "I told you before—if I wanted your attention, I'd ask for it. But I don't. I only want Shay, so you'd better make sure everyone else knows I'm off-limits. Are we clear?"

"Yeah, we're clear," she mumbled, her confidence deflated as she shuffled away.

Good. I didn't want her or anyone else trying to stir up more trouble between me and Shay.

I made my way to the bar and dropped onto a stool beside Silver. Jane caught sight of me, frowned, and got up to leave. Just fucking great. Now Jane was pissed at me too. I let out a long breath, signaling the prospect for a beer. Planting my elbows on the bar, I dropped my head into my hands.

"Having a rough night, son?" Silver's voice rumbled beside me, calm and gravelly, like he'd seen this all before.

"You could say that," I muttered. "How can one fuckup cause so much goddamn trouble?"

Silver let out a deep laugh, his lips curling under that impressive mustache. If Sam Elliott had a long-lost twin, it was him. The man was solid, wise, and hard as nails.

"Depends on what the fuckup is," he said, taking a swig of his drink. "From what I've heard, screwing around with another woman when you're into Shay? Yeah, that's a pretty big fuckup."

I groaned, rubbing the back of my neck. "It wasn't like that. I didn't fuck that another woman. I was just in my head, and I... I stopped before anything happened. But now Shay won't forgive me."

Silver leaned back on his stool, his pale blue eyes steady and thoughtful. "You gotta remember where Shay comes from, Fuse. She grew up watching her old man pull that same bullshit on Jane. I loved Shupp—he was my brother—but he was a goddamn fool when it came to his ol' lady. He loved Jane, no doubt about it, but he couldn't keep his dick in his pants. He cried into his beer more nights than I can count over how she wouldn't forgive him. But did he stop? Hell no."

I stayed silent, listening.

Silver continued, his voice softer now. "After Shupp died, I knew I wanted Jane. So I cut ties with the other women—completely. For years, I proved to her that I wasn't like him. I showed her I could be loyal, even before I made a move. Then, of course, I got sent to the pen for a few years, but I never forgot that vow. When I got out, I picked up right where I left off. You get to my age, Fuse, and random pussy don't mean shit. It's about intimacy. Connection. That's the real prize."

"Shadow said something like that," I admitted, frowning into my beer. "He's got it all under control. I don't know how he does it, but he's rock solid with Mary."

Silver let out a chuckle. "Shadow's got the right idea. I like the direction he's taking the club, too. Keeping the wilder shit behind closed doors? It lets men bring their ol' ladies around without them watching the free-for-all. If I wanna see that kind of action, Jane and I handle it in private." He laughed again, a gruff, warm sound.

"Jesus, too much information, Silver," I grumbled, shaking my head. But I couldn't deny he was right. I'd fought Shadow's changes at first, but now I saw the value in them.

Silver stood, his chair scraping against the floor. "If you want Shay, you'll have to play dirty. She's a tough one, but I think you can handle her." He patted my shoulder and headed off toward Jane, leaving me with that nugget of wisdom.

I barely had time to process what he'd said when I heard a voice behind me.

"Hey, asshole!"

I turned to see Black stalking toward me, looking about ready to throw down. "What's your problem now?" I asked, smirking as he stopped next to me.

"You know damn well what my problem is," he snapped. "That flighty bitch Kim wouldn't leave me alone all night. She was like a goddamn octopus. I know you sent her after me."

I shrugged, feigning innocence. "She just wanted to cheer you up. You seemed down, brother."

"Bullshit. You owe me for that." He flicked me off, turning to leave. "You caused me to miss Shay tonight, and I'm not forgetting that."

I watched him walk out, a satisfied grin tugging at my lips. He'd deal, and I didn't regret it one bit, brother or not.

Silver's words played again in my head. *If you want Shay, you'll have to play dirty.* And just like that, a plan started to form. I knew what I had to do, and the first part of that plan? It would start tonight.

16

I slowly started waking up, and immediately I realized I was not in bed alone. Instead, a warm body snuggled up to me, an arm and leg thrown over my body, trapping me. I knew it was Fuse without turning over and, aside from his unique smell, his tattoos gave it away.

What the hell?

A surge of panic and anger pulsed through me as I felt his body against mine. His lips on my hair, his erection pressed into my back, trapping me.

"Get off me," I growled, trying to push him away. But Fuse was too strong, too determined.

"I had to see you, little rockstar," he whispered in my ear. "I can't stay away from you."

"How did you even get in here?" I demanded, my muscles tensed with resistance.

"That lock on your door doesn't mean shit to me. You can't keep me out," Fuse said, his hands running down my body.

"You're insane. And delusional. I'm not falling for this again," I spat.

"Oh, but you already have, Shay. You've taken over my mind and body. My cock recognizes no one else," Fuse breathed, turning me onto my back and pinning me down with his weight.

I looked up into his smoldering amber eyes, torn between arousal and anger.

"Don't play games with me," I hissed, trying to push him off. "You were doing this same shit with that club woman the other night. Your dick recognized her just fine, so don't bullshit me."

But Fuse didn't budge, only raised himself on his elbows to gaze down at me. "It's not a game, baby. You know it. Every time I think of you, I get hard. That club bitch didn't do shit for me. I wouldn't have fucked her, and I think deep down you know I'm telling the truth."

I scoffed, "How am I supposed to believe that? And even if it's true, how can I trust you after what you did?"

"I know I have to earn your trust back. And I will do whatever it takes," Fuse promised.

My heart ached at the thought of losing him, but my mind screamed self-preservation. "I can't just forget what happened and start over."

"Please, just give me a chance." He leaned down to kiss me softly, and I couldn't resist kissing him back. "If after a week you find it's not happening, then you can tell me to get lost."

"Okay," I relented, hating myself for giving in so easily. "But I'm not making any promises."

"That's all I ask." Fuse kissed me again before getting up and quickly getting dressed. My body screamed for him to stay, to make love to me, but my mind knew better.

As he left for church, I lay in bed, fighting the temptation to chase after him. This man was going to be the death of me. And I couldn't resist him. It was like a drug, and I was hopelessly addicted.

I felt like a weight had been lifted off me. Shay was at least talking to me again and willing to give me a chance. That was more than I thought I'd get this soon. Sitting in the meeting room, I waited for church to start, my mind running a mile a minute. I was early, absently watching as the rest of the brothers filed in. Shadow had called for every club member to be here this morning.

That was never a good sign.

Something had gone down.

Shadow wasted no time, his voice sharp and steady as he started the meeting. "Domino called in late last night. When they got to the drop, someone opened fire. Runner was shot. Domino and Johnny handled the shooter, but Runner's at Panther's clubhouse in Sarasota getting medical treatment. No word yet on how the surgery went."

"What the fuck?" Vampire barked, scowling. "This shit cannot stand. We need to take action."

Viking jumped in, his voice calm but cutting. "Moreno, what's the update on the prospect Tommy? First, we find the rat. If it's him, he's dead."

"I've been tailing him all week," Moreno answered, shaking his head. "So far, I can't pin anything on him. I even searched his room—nothing. Maybe we're wrong about him."

Kickstand spoke up, his tone frustrated. "I've swept the whole clubhouse for bugs. Found nothing. Someone has to be feeding information to the Fire Dragons."

Shadow's gaze was ice-cold as he scanned the room, his voice low and deadly. "Let me be clear. I'm not saying there's a rat in this room, but I am saying this: when we find him, his death will be slow and painful."

Silence settled like a heavy fog.

I broke it. "Do you think what happened to Shay could be related?"

That got everyone's attention.

"What happened to Shay?" Black asked, his eyes narrowing.

"Someone's been leaving her threatening notes. Last night, they trashed her car—took a bat to it, smashed the windows, flattened the tires. Total loss."

Kickstand piped up again. "I checked all the security feeds. There's no camera in the hall by the backstage rooms, so I fixed that this morning. The person who destroyed her car covered their face, so we couldn't make anything out from the video."

"Fuse, you sure it couldn't be one of your jealous exes?" Vampire asked, smirking.

"How the hell should I know?" I shot back, my patience thinning. "But my gut tells me no. This feels like something else."

"I agree," Shadow said, his tone serious. "The figure on the feed was a man. This isn't some jealous woman. Is it related to Cross and the Fire Dragons? I don't know, but until we figure it out, Shay needs to be guarded."

"I'll do it," Black volunteered immediately.

"The fuck you will," I growled, stepping forward. "I'll take care of my woman."

Black squared up to me, eyes blazing. "*Your woman?* Everyone knows you fucked some chick at Patch's. You don't deserve Shay."

"Why the fuck is my business all over the club?" I snapped, glaring around the room. "We gossiping like old ladies now? For the last time, I didn't do shit. Keep my name out of your mouths. Shay and

I talked, and she's fine with me watching her."

"Jesus Christ, both of you shut the fuck up," Shadow barked, slamming his hand on the table. "Fuse, you're on Shay. But if she has a problem with it, we'll switch out. End of discussion."

I bit back the urge to keep arguing, even as Black shot me a glare that promised we weren't done.

Viking spoke up, breaking the tension. "We need to prepare for a lockdown. Start moving your women and kids to the clubhouse now. It'll be easier to keep everyone safe if shit goes south."

Shadow added, "Mary volunteered to homeschool the kids while they're here. If anyone isn't comfortable sending their kids to school during this, let Viking know. This goes for anyone's ol' lady who works—put someone on them for security. It's better to have all the families in one place."

"Keep your weapons on you at all times," Vampire said, looking around the room. "Watch for anything suspicious. From what we know, Cross hasn't been seen in weeks. That could mean he's closer than we think."

Shadow stood, wrapping things up. "Church again on Wednesday at six. Everyone better be here. Meeting adjourned."

As soon as I stepped out of the room, Black was waiting for me, his fists clenched at his sides. "You'll fuck up, Fuse. There's not a chance in hell you'll keep your cock in your pants. You don't deserve Shay." His voice was low and hard before he turned and walked off without giving me a chance to respond.

I watched him go, my jaw tight. Willing myself to stay calm and not fucking explode, but Black was testing me, pushing me to the edge. I knew I'd earned my reputation, but fuck it all, I wasn't that guy anymore.

She made me want to be better. I loved her.

17

Sitting at breakfast with Mom and Mary, I sipped my coffee, trying to push away my lingering thoughts from last night. The men started to file in, their boots thudding against the wood floor, and I wasn't surprised when Black dropped into the seat beside me. What did surprise me, though, was his apology.

"I'm sorry about last night, Shay. Some chick glued herself to me. Someone told her I needed cheering up because my girlfriend dumped me." Black smirked, but I could see the irritation in his eyes.

I didn't need to guess who that *someone* was. *Fuse.* I should have known he'd pull something to sabotage my plans with Black. Typical.

"It's okay, Black," I replied, brushing it off. "With someone smashing my car to pieces, I wouldn't have been in the mood anyway."

His expression darkened, his easygoing demeanor replaced with hard edges. "Yeah, I heard about that. It's bullshit. Don't worry—we'll catch whoever did it. They'll pay for messing with you." Then, softening again, he grinned. "So, how about a rain check on that drink?"

Before I could respond, a familiar voice cut in. "Hey, little rockstar."

Fuse slid onto the bench beside me and pulled me against him like I was already his. His arm settled possessively around my shoulders, and his amber eyes flicked to Black in a silent warning.

Black wasn't fazed. "Get back to me about that drink, Shay. I'll see you at your show Friday night." He stood, meeting Fuse's stare with one of his own before walking away.

I sighed, turning toward Fuse. "Was it really necessary to set him up last night?"

Fuse shrugged, not even bothering to deny it. "He told you, huh? I don't want him sniffing around you, Shay."

"You don't own me, Fuse," I shot back, poking him in the ribs for emphasis. "And maybe you need a reminder about what *you* were sniffing around the other night."

He winced at that, but his response was soft, almost teasing. "I don't want to argue, little rockstar. Let's do something today—just us. I thought we could take a ride, stop for something to eat, and come back later."

I hesitated, but the temptation was too strong to resist. The thought of the wind whipping around me, the stress melting away, and the thrill of riding with Fuse was too appealing. I felt safe with him, and right now, that meant everything.

"Sure," I said, nodding. "I'd like that. Let me get ready, and I'll meet you out front."

Fuse's face broke into a smile—one of those real smiles that made him look younger and carefree. He stood, kissing the top of my head like it was the most natural thing in the world. "See you in a few, Shay."

I watched him walk away, but I wasn't the only one. I could feel the weight of someone else's stare. Turning, I caught Lexi's narrowed eyes boring into me from across the room. She turned to whisper something to the girl beside her, and I shook my head. I could see how a guy like Fuse would pull you in. He had that rough charm, that magnetic smile. But women like Lexi knew the deal when they signed up for this life—they were just part of the game. You couldn't let your feelings get involved.

"Hey, Shay," Mary said, breaking into my thoughts. I looked at her, surprised by the genuine concern in her voice. "I know I'm not a big talker, and sometimes that makes me seem standoffish, but I mean it when I say—if you need anything, please just ask."

I smiled, touched by her kindness. "Thanks, Mary. Honestly, the only thing I need right now is a car, but I'll figure it out."

Mary tilted her head thoughtfully. "I'd offer you mine, but it's still in Florida. My dad's driving it up next month. But seriously, if you need anything—me or Shadow—we're here."

"Thanks," I said, appreciating the offer. It was strange hearing her talk about Shadow that way—like he was some approachable teddy bear instead of a mad skunk. I couldn't imagine the man as anything but intimidating.

Still, her words reminded me that I wasn't entirely alone here, even if it felt that way sometimes.

I glanced at the time and stood, brushing my hands against my jeans. "I'd better get moving. Fuse is probably already waiting."

I caught Mom's eye on my way out, her smile soft but knowing. I wasn't sure what the day would bring, but for a little while, I'd let myself forget the mess of last night and just ride.

THE DEVIL'S HOUSE
PENNSYLVANIA
FUSE

I checked the time again, a knot of unease forming in my chest. Shay wouldn't blow me off—at least, I didn't think she would. Before the doubt could settle, the door swung open, and there she was.

Damn.

It hit me every time I saw her. Shay didn't even need to try to look sexy; she just *was*. Tight jeans, a fitted T-shirt, and a pair of Vans—it was simple, but on her, it was everything. When she lifted her arms to slide into her jacket, the fabric pulled just right, and I nearly groaned.

Fuck me. Perfect.

"Hop that tight ass on, little rockstar," I said, holding out the helmet with a cocky grin.

Rolling her eyes, she shot back, "Fuse, the shit you say—how are you not slapped more often?"

I smirked. "I only speak the truth, Shay."

With an exaggerated sigh, she took the helmet and climbed onto the bike behind me. The moment her arms wrapped around my waist and her legs settled beside mine, a sense of rightness settled in my chest. I felt... whole.

Jesus, I sound like some lovesick poet.

At the gate, I revved the engine, and once the road opened up, I let my baby loose. The roar of the engine, the wind whipping past, the vibrations of the bike beneath me—it was a feeling no one could replicate. But this time, it was better with Shay's arms holding me tight.

We rode for an hour and a half, weaving through the mountains until I pulled up to the overlook I had in mind. The Italian restaurant sitting at the edge of the cliffs had the best pizza I'd ever tasted, and the view — miles of rolling mountains — was unbeatable.

Shay climbed off the bike, stretching her legs as we walked toward the overlook. She turned, smiling at me as she took in the view.

"This is incredible," she said, her tone soft, relaxed. "The ride up here was beautiful."

"There's nothing like riding through the mountains," I replied, my eyes lingering on her face longer than they should. "And the food here's good too. We'll grab a bite, then head back."

Inside, the hostess sat us by the window, where the view stretched endlessly. We ordered, and for over an hour, we ate, talked, and laughed. It surprised me how easy it was to talk to her — how I didn't feel the need to hide anything. Shay didn't expect anything from me; she just *was*, and I wanted to soak up every bit of her.

When I glanced at the time, I was surprised. "Guess we lost track."

"Guess we did," she said, her grin softening as she wiped her hands.

On the way back, the ride started as smooth as before, but something caught my attention — a truck behind us. It wasn't just following us; it was staying back, deliberate. My gut clenched.

The truck had a cage on the front — a dead giveaway. I'd seen it before when we captured those bastards.

Shit.

I tightened my grip on the bars, my mind racing. Turning down a side road, I wanted to see if they'd follow.

They did.

Motherfuckers.

My pulse kicked up a notch, but I forced myself to stay calm. I couldn't risk a confrontation — not with Shay. Taking another side road, I spotted a cluster of trees. I quickly pulled off the road, maneuvering the bike into the shadows.

"What's going on, Fuse?" Shay asked, her voice tight with confusion.

"Get off, Shay. I need to hide the bike farther in."

She jumped off quickly, her eyes darting nervously around the quiet woods.

Once the bike was tucked away in the trees, I pulled out my phone and sent a single word to the club officers: **Trouble.** They'd track us with the GPS on my phone and bike. Then, I grabbed my gun.

Turning to Shay, I softened my voice. "Stay back, away from the road. We're being tailed, and that truck will be here any second."

"I don't like this, Fuse," she said, her arms crossing tightly over her chest. "What if they see us?"

Before I could answer, the low rumble of an engine cut through the silence. We both crouched low as the truck crept along the road, its tinted windows making it impossible to see inside.

They know we're close.

The truck moved slowly, scanning the treeline. I pushed the bike back farther and pulled Shay behind it, shielding her from view.

"I let the club know what's going on," I whispered. "They're on their way. Shouldn't be more than half an hour."

"I hope you're right," Shay murmured. She held herself tightly, her voice trembling. "This shit scares me."

"Don't worry. They won't find us unless we move, and I'm not letting that happen. Help's coming."

Fifteen minutes passed like hours. Then came the first gunshots.

Fuck.

The truck doubled back, this time firing randomly into the trees. I pulled Shay down, covering her with my body.

"Stay down!" I barked. I heard her sharp intake of breath as another shot cracked through the air, hitting my bike with a dull *thud*.

I ground my teeth, furious. "These assholes just fucked up," I muttered under my breath.

The truck inched forward again, but then I heard the sound I'd been waiting for—the growl of motorcycle engines.

My brothers were here.

The truck's engine revved, tires screeching as it sped off. I stood, turning to Shay. "Stay here. I'll be right back."

I ran to the road in time to see ten of my brothers surrounding the truck up ahead. Gunfire rang out again, but it was short-lived. By the time I caught up, the truck was stopped, and Vampire and Stonewall were cautiously approaching the doors.

Vampire peered through the window and called out, "It's clear. Only two men."

Shadow turned to me as I approached. "You and Shay okay?"

"Yeah," I said, exhaling hard. "I noticed them early and got us out of sight. My bike took a hit, but nothing major."

"Good call." Shadow nodded, his expression hard as he glanced at the truck. "Shame we couldn't get more out of them, but the assholes kept firing."

I turned just as Shay walked up beside me, her eyes wide as she took in the scene. "What did they want?" she asked.

"I don't know," I admitted, steering her away. "I'm just glad we got out of sight when we did."

Shadow caught my eye and gave a slight nod, letting me know he'd handle the mess.

"Come on, Shay," I said, taking her hand. "Let's go check the bike and see what damage that bullet did."

I led her away, relieved to get her clear of the mess. I'd been ready to fight, but now all I wanted was to get Shay somewhere safe—and keep her there.

I was doing my best to stay calm, but the shit that just went down had me shaken. On top of that, Fuse wasn't telling me a damn thing.

He rolled his bike back onto the road, crouching down to inspect the damage. The bullet had punched a hole clean through the fender, but it wasn't much else—cosmetic damage at most. Satisfied, Fuse swung his leg over the bike and glanced back at me.

"Hop on, Shay."

I climbed on behind him, wrapping my arms tightly around his waist. As we rounded the curve, the ditch where the truck had landed earlier came into view. It was already empty. One of the men was driving the truck, now loaded up with a motorcycle on the back.

They work fast, I thought, unnerved. Almost like they did this sort of thing every day.

The club men mounted their bikes with practiced precision. Shadow gave the signal, and we took off, heading back to the clubhouse.

As I pressed into Fuse's back, my thoughts started spinning. The violence I'd just witnessed wasn't something I could shrug off. It wasn't just the women and the party scene that made me wary of this life—it was moments like these. Moments where you didn't get answers. Moments where you were scared shitless and expected to just deal with it.

Fuse took a sharp curve, and I instinctively tightened my hold, leaning with him. God help me, even now, I loved the way this felt—being close to him, feeling safe in this fleeting moment of chaos.

Why does it have to feel this good?

For two years, I'd been with Shawn, and when I walked away, it was my pride that hurt more than my heart. But Fuse? I'd known him for weeks, and the thought of leaving him in a few months felt like my heart was breaking already.

Better to leave than be left, I reminded myself.

When we pulled up in front of the clubhouse, Fuse stopped the bike, and I swung my leg off, trying to shake off my unease. Fuse stayed seated, keeping one hand on the throttle while his other reached out to brush my cheek. His touch was soft, completely at odds with the rough biker persona he wore like armor.

"I'll put my bike in the garage," he murmured, his amber eyes holding mine. "I'll be right in."

I nodded, unable to find my voice.

Heading inside, I barely made it through the door before Mom rushed at me, pulling me into her arms.

"Shay, are you okay? I was so worried." Her voice trembled with relief. "I think you should stay inside the clubhouse until whatever this is gets sorted."

I pulled back gently, trying to reassure her. "Mom, I can't. I have to practice and perform. It's my job, and I'll be fine—I won't be alone, I promise."

Her face crumpled in worry. "Shay, promise me you'll be extra cautious. I don't know what I'd do if something happened to you."

The fear in her eyes hit me hard, and guilt settled like a stone in my chest. I tucked a strand of her hair behind her ear and nodded. "I promise. I'll be careful. Really, Mom."

Her shoulders sagged a little with relief.

"Now," I said, forcing a smile, "I need to pee and get something to eat before I collapse. I'll be back down in a few minutes, okay?"

Mom reluctantly let me go, watching me as I walked toward the stairs.

The moment I hit the hallway, my confident front slipped. My mom wasn't wrong to worry—I was worried too. Someone had targeted me. My car was totaled, I was getting threats, and worst of all, no one seemed to have answers.

It's scary as hell.

But I hadn't lied to her. I *would* be careful. I'd make sure someone was always with me, and if that meant having someone in my bed too, so be it.

Because whatever was happening, I wasn't going to let it break me.

18

As I wheeled my bike into the garage, I couldn't help but feel a sense of unease. Shadow and Vampire stood nearby, their body language tense and alert.

"Are you calling church, Shadow?" I asked, wondering if we would have an emergency meeting.

"No, not yet," Shadow replied, his jaw set in determination. "We need more information before we make any moves. Our safety plans are already in motion."

Vampire chimed in with his own question. "How did someone know you were out on a ride today, Fuse?"

I racked my brain but couldn't come up with an answer. "I have no idea. I didn't see anyone following us on the way up, only on the way back."

"I don't like this. It's possible we're being watched," Shadow said, furrowing his brow in thought. "Vampire, gather a group and investigate the wooded area around the club."

"Do you need me to come along?" I offered.

"No, you go inside. Shay had a shock today, and she needs to talk to you," Vampire replied.

Relieved that I wouldn't have to join the investigation, I headed inside the clubhouse. As soon as I reached Shay's room, I let out a sigh of relief when I found the door unlocked. The sound of running water caught my attention, and I realized Shay must be taking a shower.

Perfect timing.

Quickly undressing, my cock already hard at the thought of fucking Shay in the shower, I made my way into the bathroom. Seeing her naked body under the spray of water made my cock jump even more. God, I loved her small and curvy body and watching her hands glide over it as she washed was enough to make me lose control.

Without warning, I opened the shower door and stepped inside, causing Shay to let out a startled scream. "What the fuck, Fuse? I'm going to kill you!" she yelled, her eyes wide with shock.

But I didn't give her a chance to react. Pushing her against the wall, I pressed my body against her and claimed her lips in a heated kiss. Our tongues tangled while I ground my straining cock against her stomach. My hands found their way to her breasts, squeezing and pinching her nipples until she let out a guttural groan of pleasure.

Suddenly, Shay pushed me back and dropped to her knees. Looking up at me with desire-filled eyes, she stuck out her tongue and licked the precum from the tip of my dick. It was almost enough to make me explode right then and there.

Not breaking our intense eye contact, Shay took me into her mouth and began sucking on me hungrily. I couldn't help but grab a handful of her hair and guide her head up and down on my throbbing cock. Seeing her other hand slip between her legs, playing with herself as she pleasured me only added to my arousal.

With each passing second, the pleasure grew more intense until I couldn't hold back any longer. As Shay continued to suck on me like her favorite candy, I decided I needed to be inside her.

With a swift movement, I lifted her up and pressed her back against the cool, tiled wall. Her legs instinctively wrapped around my waist as I thrust into her, feeling her body open up to me in response. The sounds of our pleasure reverberated off the bathroom walls, filling the small space with echoes of moans and gasps.

My hips moved at a frenzied pace, driving deep inside of her with each powerful thrust. Shay's moans grew louder and her hips began to move faster in time with my own. My hand found its way to her clit, rubbing and teasing it until she couldn't hold back any longer. With a scream of pleasure, Shay reached her orgasm, and I could feel her muscles contracting around me.

In that moment, I felt my own release building, my balls tightening as I let out a primal roar. I exploded inside of her, my cock pulsating as my hot cum shot deep into her pussy. We stayed connected as we caught our breaths, basking in the overwhelming sensations we had just shared.

Shay ran her hands soothingly up and down my back as I pulled away slightly to look into her eyes. She was addicting, I thought to myself, unable to tear my gaze away from her. Our connection went beyond just physical pleasure; there was something deeper between us and I knew she felt it too.

But then Shay whispered something that broke through the post-orgasmic haze we were both in. "Fuse, I hate to break the afterglow, but you didn't use a condom."

"Shit," I cursed under my breath, suddenly remembering the condom sitting on the sink. "I'm sorry, Shay. I brought one with me, but in the heat of the moment, I forgot." It wasn't like me to have unprotected sex; I always made sure to use condoms. But with Shay, I had lost control and gave in to the incredible sensation of going bareback. It was unlike anything I had ever experienced.

But then another thought hit me. "Shay, are you on birth control?" I asked, suddenly feeling a wave of panic wash over me.

She shook her head, looking just as panicked as I felt. "I haven't needed it in two years," she admitted. "I skipped my last appointment because I didn't plan on having sex with anyone."

My mind raced with the implications. Two years? I never would have guessed. And surprisingly, the idea of potentially getting her pregnant didn't scare me like it should have. In fact, a small part of me felt excited at the prospect of starting a family with Shay. But before I could dwell on it any further, Shay spoke up again.

"It was only this one time and I'm sure nothing will happen," she said, sounding hopeful.

I nodded reassuringly. "Whatever happens, happens. We'll deal with it together," I promised, surprising even myself with my calm response.

But then Shay reminded me that we were still standing in a cold shower, and I realized we needed to get out and get dressed. Reluctantly, I let her down, and we quickly washed off before drying off and getting dressed. The events of our steamy encounter lingered in our minds as we went about the rest of our day, leaving us both wondering what the future held for us.

"I'm starving; let's get something to eat, little rockstar."

"I'm hungry too. I figured a quick shower, then food. I never expected to find a biker in my shower set on ravishing me," she laughed.

"Shay, baby, get used to it. I'm not going anywhere," I told her as I grabbed her hand, pulling her out the door.

19

I decided I wouldn't overthink the future—I'd focus on the present. The thought of getting pregnant wasn't something I wanted to consider right now. Sure, I could blame it all on Fuse, but I'd gotten caught up in the moment too. *Fuck it*. I wanted Fuse, and I was tired of fighting it.

Still, I felt like one of those women in romance novels who jump back in with the guy while the reader is screaming, *"Don't do it! He'll only hurt you again."*

"What are you thinking about?" Fuse murmured, his voice low as he leaned into me. He licked my earlobe, sending a shiver down my spine.

We were sitting at the bar, sharing a drink after dinner. The clubhouse was alive for a Sunday evening—nothing says "Sunday relaxation" like Five Finger Death Punch blaring from the speakers. At least twenty club members were scattered around, playing pool, talking, or entertaining club girls draped across their laps.

I took a sip of my drink, suddenly feeling bold. "Can I ask you something? And you have to promise to answer truthfully."

Fuse paused, his amber eyes narrowing as he considered me. "This sounds like one of those trick questions. But go ahead."

I held his gaze. "Was the allure of the club girls one of the reasons you joined the club?"

Fuse leaned back slightly, his expression thoughtful. He chose his words carefully. "Honestly, Shay, no. I didn't join for the club girls. I joined for the brotherhood. Before I found the club, I was on my way to jail—or worse. Hoss took me under his wing, gave me a purpose, and saved my damn life. I never had a real family. My mom took off when I was a kid, leaving my old man to raise me... and trust me, he sucked at it."

He paused, his tone steady. "The club gave me people who would have my back for the first time in my life. A family. The club girls? They were just part of the scene. I was single, so yeah, I took advantage of it. But they weren't why I joined."

I nodded, chewing on his words. "I'm trying to understand. My dad—he couldn't help himself when it came to the younger, sexier women. It was too easy for him, and it destroyed my mom. I like you, Fuse. A lot. But I worry... what if the same thing happens down the line? Men don't always think with their heads, and it's just so easy here—too easy."

My voice cracked as I looked away. "I don't want to end up like my mom. I love her, but I always wished she would stand up for herself. I'm not even making sense." I sighed, feeling suddenly small.

"Look at me, Shay." Fuse's voice was soft but commanding. He gently turned my face toward him, forcing me to meet his eyes. "Not all men are like that. *I'm not like that.* I promise you, if you don't kick me to the curb, I'll never go to those club parties without you. I know how wild they get, and I wouldn't put you through that. I would never cheat on you. My childhood sucked, and I saw firsthand what that shit does to a family. I won't be that guy."

"What about the other night?" My voice was quiet, but the hurt lingered in my tone. "You were drunk, Fuse. You tried being with that woman."

"Shay," he said, exhaling heavily. "I swear to you, I wasn't even fucking interested. My head was a mess—so wrapped up thinking about you and what I feel for you that I couldn't think straight. I wasn't focused on her at all. It was a mistake, and I'm not drinking like that again. At least, not without you by my side."

I studied him for a long moment, searching for cracks in his words. "I swear to you, Fuse," I said slowly, "if I give you another chance and you screw up, I will cut off your dick and shove it down your lying throat!"

He chuckled, though there was no humor in it. "That's brutal as shit, Shay. Warning noted."

I stood, brushing my hands down the front of my jeans. "I'm gonna go see my mom. She's probably worried sick after everything that happened today."

Fuse pulled me into him, his arms strong and sure around my waist. He kissed me softly, lingering just long enough to make my pulse race. "Okay," he murmured against my lips. "I'll swing by your room later for bedtime." He winked and turned toward the back of the clubhouse, leaving me with my thoughts.

I watched him walk away, my heart betraying me with its rapid beat. I hoped I was doing the right thing. I *wanted* to believe him, but time would tell.

It always did.

I was one lucky bastard. I never thought Shay would give me another chance after the colossal fuck-up I pulled, but here I was. I wasn't about to mess it up again. Not this time.

Heading out to check on my bike, I froze mid-step when I noticed the prospect, Tommy, slipping out of the storage room. My eyes narrowed. That room *always* stayed locked unless it was needed, and it just so happened to sit right next to the chapel where we held church.

Tommy had no damn business in there.

I stayed hidden, watching as he turned the corner and headed outside like he didn't have a care in the world. The moment he was out of sight, I walked straight to the door and grabbed the handle. Locked. Just as I figured.

"Stonewall," I called, spotting him coming down the hall. "Got a sec?"

"What's up?" Stonewall's brow furrowed as he strolled over, his usual cocky swagger in place.

"Come with me," I said, lowering my voice. "In the storage room."

He raised a brow, smirking. "What the fuck, Fuse? You're not my type, man."

"Ha, ha. Funny asshole," I muttered, rolling my eyes. "This is serious. I think Tommy's up to something."

Stonewall's expression sobered instantly. I unlocked the door, and we both stepped inside. The room smelled faintly of dust, racks of tools and supplies lining the walls.

"What did you see?" Stonewall asked, his voice now as low as mine.

"I caught Tommy coming out of here. He shouldn't be in this room, and my gut tells me we need to look around."

"Logical place to start is the wall separating this room from the chapel." Stonewall motioned with his chin.

We got to work, pulling the racks away from the wall and shining our phone flashlights into the tight space. It didn't take long.

"Son of a bitch," Stonewall hissed, holding his light steady. Embedded in the wall was a small hole. Hidden inside was a recorder—complete with Bluetooth capabilities.

I pulled the device out, holding it up like it was evidence in a crime scene. "It's battery operated," I said, inspecting it. "But he probably swapped out the batteries whenever he needed. How long do you think this has been here?"

"Too long," Stonewall muttered, cracking his knuckles. "I'll tell you this much—Tommy's not walking away from this clean."

"We need to take this to Shadow," I said, slipping the recorder into my pocket. "Now."

We left the storage room and made our way to Shadow's office. I knocked once, hard, before hearing Shadow's voice.

"Enter."

I pushed the door open, stepping in with Stonewall close behind. Mary was standing by the desk, cheeks flushed and eyes wide. Shadow's expression said we interrupted something.

"Hey, Lenny. Hey, Fuse. I'll leave you guys to it," Mary said quickly, practically darting for the door.

"Great fucking timing," Shadow muttered, settling back into his chair. His gaze shifted to us, sharp and expectant. "What's going on?"

I didn't waste time. Pulling the recorder from my pocket, I tossed it onto his desk. "Found this in the storage room next to the chapel. I saw Tommy coming out of there earlier."

Shadow's jaw ticked as he stared at the recorder. The silence was deafening for a second before Stonewall broke it.

"The rat is Tommy for sure," Stonewall said, his voice hard.

Shadow's fist slammed onto the desk, rattling everything on it. "I want him in the basement," he growled, his tone pure fury. "We won't lay a hand on him tonight—let the fucker sweat it out and think about what's coming. Tomorrow, Viking, Vampire, and I will take him apart and get the answers we need."

I nodded, already itching to drag Tommy's sorry ass downstairs.

"Fuse and I will grab him now," Stonewall said, his fists clenching. "We'll put him in room two. But it's going to take a lot of goddamn restraint for me not to rearrange his face on the way down."

Shadow's glare shot to me. "You make sure he doesn't lose control, Fuse."

I huffed out a breath. "Will do. We'll handle it, Shadow."

Stonewall and I turned to leave. As we stepped into the hallway, Stonewall cracked his neck, his eyes full of fire.

"I swear to God, Fuse, if that little shit even looks at me sideways, I'm gonna—"

"Rein it in," I cut him off, my tone firm. "We'll get him downstairs, no more, no less. Then Shadow can decide how to handle the rest."

"Yeah, yeah." Stonewall waved me off, but the tension in his shoulders told me he was wound tight.

Tommy had no idea what he'd gotten himself into.

We were going to find him. And when we did, he'd regret the day he ever betrayed this club.

20

True to his word, Fuse showed up at my door for "bedtime," promising to rock my world just like I rocked his—and, damn it, he did.

This morning, we had breakfast together before he headed out to the garage. I had band practice at noon, and Fuse said he'd pick me up when it was time. That left me a couple of hours to kill.

I spent the morning in the bar area, talking with Mary, Joe, and Lettie, who were now staying at the clubhouse because of the possible threat. Joe had three kids—two rambunctious boys and a little girl, the youngest, who sat contentedly on her lap. She couldn't have been more than two years old, with chubby cheeks and big brown eyes that made her look like a porcelain doll.

Watching them play tug-of-war with a stuffed animal, I couldn't help but wonder: *What if I got pregnant?* The thought sent my mind spinning. Me. A mom. I was twenty-eight and mature enough to handle it... right? But I couldn't picture it—couldn't picture myself holding a tiny baby in my arms. Would Fuse even want that kind of life? I shook the thought away, telling myself not to overthink.

By the time eleven-thirty rolled around, I went up to get ready, slipping into my favorite jeans and a loose top, before heading outside to wait for Fuse.

It wasn't long before I heard the familiar rumble of his motorcycle approaching. He pulled up, a smug smile already on his face, as he pulled out a helmet and handed it to me.

"Hop on, little rockstar," he said, his tone teasing and easy. "Unless your pussy is too sore from the pounding I gave it last night."

"You have a dirty mouth, Fuse," I shot back, smirking. "And maybe my pussy didn't even know your dick was there."

"That so?" He leaned in just a little, his voice dropping to a husky murmur. "Guess I'll have to pound extra hard tonight. Now, hop on."

Rolling my eyes—and trying not to grin too hard—I climbed on the back of his bike. My body was still sore, but there was no way in hell I'd admit that to him. Cocky bastard would never let me live it down.

Fuse parked behind *The Unlimited*, walking me inside with a casual confidence that always seemed to surround him. The rest of the band was already there, tuning guitars and setting up amps. Fuse shot me a wink before turning to leave.

"I'll be back in three hours. Try not to miss me too much," he said, walking off with his usual swagger.

"You're so full of yourself," I called after him, earning a laugh over his shoulder as he disappeared out the door.

Band practice went off without a hitch at first. We were locked in, playing harder and tighter than we had in weeks. Midway through, we took a much-needed break, and Gabe mentioned a vintage guitar he'd scored.

"You've *got* to see this thing," he said, excitement lighting up his face. "It's in my car."

Curiosity piqued, Mark, Steve, and I followed him out back. Gabe was practically bouncing as he led us toward his old beat-up sedan, digging into his jacket like he was reaching for his keys.

What happened next felt like a nightmare in slow motion.

"I didn't want to do this," Gabe said, his voice low and strained, "but I had no choice."

He pulled a gun.

My blood turned to ice.

"Gabe, what the hell?" Mark growled, raising his hands in reflex. Steve froze beside me, his mouth falling open in shock.

Before I could even scream, a black van screeched around the corner, slamming to a stop. Doors flew open, and three masked men jumped out.

"Run—" I barely got the word out before they were on us.

One man grabbed me from behind, an arm like a steel band locking around my waist. I kicked and twisted, but it was useless. My heart thundered in my chest as panic set in.

"Let me go!" I screamed, struggling against him.

A flash of movement—Steve going for one of the men—was met with the sickening sound of a fist colliding with flesh. I heard Mark yell something, but I couldn't make out the words.

"Shay!"

A sharp blow struck the back of my head, and the world tilted. I felt myself being dragged, the gravel biting into my shoes, before everything went dark.

21

I was about to head back to pick up Shay when my phone buzzed. The screen lit up with a message from Kickstand: *Get back to the bar. Now.*

No explanation.

My stomach dropped like a lead weight. A group text meant whatever had happened wasn't minor.

I jumped on my bike, firing it up without hesitation, and tore back to *The Unlimited*. By the time I got there, all the club officers were already gathered outside, their faces grim and serious. My heart hammered in my chest, but I didn't see Shay anywhere.

Fuck.

"What's going on?" I barked, my voice sharp with panic.

"First off, Fuse, you need to stay calm," Shadow warned, his tone hard as steel. "Losing your shit won't help her."

I forced myself to take a breath, my hands clenching at my sides. "Tell me what happened."

Kickstand stepped forward, his voice low but steady as he laid it out. "Shay and the rest of her band went outside during their break. Reader noticed and followed, but by the time he got there, a van was already pulling up. Three men jumped out and grabbed them. From the security footage, it looks like one of the band members—Gabe—pulled a gun on the others just seconds before the van stopped."

My brain stalled. "What? Gabe? Why the hell would he do that? What do they want with the whole band?"

Shadow chimed in, his face dark. "That's the question we don't have an answer for. About an hour ago, Tommy cracked and spilled everything. Turns out he knew something big was coming—Cross is involved, along with a cop from Maryland and someone in the band. How it all connects? We're still piecing it together."

"Tommy didn't know much more," Viking added, his voice rough with frustration. "He's just been running messages for Cross. A fucking grunt."

I scrubbed a hand over my face, my chest tightening with helplessness. "Can't we track Shay somehow?"

Kickstand shook his head without looking up from his laptop. "No. She didn't have her phone on her. We searched backstage—only Gabe had his phone when they went out. I'm tracking it now, trying to get a location. Give me a minute."

A minute? I didn't have a fucking minute. My thoughts spiraled. They could be doing anything to Shay right now.

Stonewall broke through my panic. "What about Gabe's car? Is it still here?"

Reader nodded. "Yeah, it's still parked out back. He left with the others in the van."

"Let's check it out," Stonewall said, already turning toward the back lot. "Maybe we'll find something that points us in the right direction. It's worth a shot."

The rest of us followed him outside. Sure enough, Gabe's car sat like a piece of junk where he left it. Locked, of course. Stonewall didn't hesitate—he broke the window with his elbow, glass shattering onto the ground.

The inside of the car was a disaster. Empty takeout boxes, dirty clothes, crumpled receipts—it looked like a tornado had hit it.

"This guy's a pig," Stonewall muttered, rummaging through the trash in the back seat.

I leaned over, shoving a stack of napkins and wrappers off the passenger seat. That's when I saw something odd. I snatched up a handful of paper, flipping through them.

"Hey, look at this."

The others turned toward me as I held up a small stack of receipts.

"What is it?" Shadow asked.

"Receipts from a convenience store," I said, frowning. "It's way out near the industrial zone—nothing out there but abandoned factories."

Stonewall's brows furrowed. "Why the hell would he be out there? Gabe's not even from around here. There's no reason for him to go to that area."

"That's exactly what I'm thinking," I said, my pulse quickening. "What if that's where they took Shay and the band?"

Shadow nodded, his expression hardening. "It's a solid lead. Let's head back to the clubhouse, gear up, and ride out. If Kickstand gets a location on Gabe's phone, he'll update us."

Vampire grunted in agreement. "At least it's better than sitting around on our asses."

"Hell yes," I said, already straddling my bike. I couldn't stay still any longer. The thought of Shay in the hands of those bastards made my blood boil.

Shadow gave the signal, and we all took off toward the clubhouse. My bike roared beneath me, but my thoughts were a chaotic mess. Images of Shay—scared, hurt—flashed through my mind.

I wouldn't let it happen.

We'd find her.

And when we did, whoever had touched her would fucking pay.

22

My mind was struggling to emerge from the murky depths of confusion and disorientation. It felt like I was trying to climb through a thick fog, my thoughts slow and muddled. My mouth was dry and parched, as if stuffed with cotton. With great effort, I managed to pry open my heavy eyelids, taking in my surroundings. The first thing I noticed was the dim lighting and the musty smell of an old warehouse. Panic began to rise within me as I realized I had no recollection of how I got here or why.

My gaze landed on two familiar faces - Mark and Steve, fellow band members - both unconscious and bound with ropes.

What the hell was going on?

Struggling against the restraints that held me captive, I tried to sit up, but only succeeded in shifting my position against the cold, hard wall behind me. The room was empty except for some dilapidated equipment, clearly unused for quite some time. There was only one exit - a door that seemed impossibly far out of reach - and high windows that offered no hope of escape.

As Mark began to stir awake, his eyes darting around like mine in an attempt to make sense of our situation, he asked desperately, "What's happening, Shay?"

"I have no idea," I replied truthfully, feeling just as lost and terrified as he did.

"What's going on with Gabe? Why would he do this?" Mark exclaimed, looking around for him.

Before we could speculate further, the door swung open and Gabe entered with another man by his side. My heart sunk when I recognized him as a member of the "Fire Dragons".

This was bad news.

Gabe's expression showed a hint of remorse as he spoke, "I'm sorry guys, I didn't want it to come to this."

"What exactly is this, Gabe?" I demanded, my voice shaking with fear and anger.

"Cross, the president of the Fire Dragons, is my cousin. He gave me a choice - either betray you or die," Gabe explained, his own desperation evident in his eyes. It was hard to believe that someone we trusted could turn out to be so different from who we thought they were.

The other man, known as "Mouth," interjected harshly, "Don't tell them shit, Gabe."

Mouth sauntered over to where I was sitting, crouching down in front of me. His gaze roamed over my body in a way that made my skin crawl. "You're a pretty little thing, aren't you? I wouldn't mind getting my hands on you," he sneered, noticing my disgusted expression. "No need to worry though, sweetheart. I was told not to touch you unless you give us a reason. Want to give me a reason?"

Despite the fear coursing through me and the urge to fight back against this disgusting man, I knew better than to provoke him. So I stayed silent, keeping my thoughts to myself even as Mouth continued to taunt me.

"That's what I thought," he said smugly before standing back up and addressing Gabe again. "Give them some water, but keep them tied up."

Gabe fetched some bottles of water from a nearby cooler and handed them out to each of us without untying our hands. As he leaned down to whisper something in my ear, I couldn't help but feel betrayed by the friend I had once trusted.

"I tried to warn you," he murmured before moving on to Mark and Steve, who were both regaining consciousness now. I couldn't understand why the entire band was here. Why not just take me?

The confusion and fear within me continued to grow as I struggled to make sense of this nightmare. All I could do was hope that Fuse would find me soon before things took a turn for the worse.

Come on, Fuse, please find me.

Back at the clubhouse, we loaded up the van with weapons, found a prospect to drive, and geared ourselves for what was coming. Ten of us rolled out without wasting a single second. Every minute mattered. Every second counted.

If anyone touched Shay, I'd make sure they paid—no, they'd pay anyway for taking her. In such a short time, she'd become something I didn't even know I needed—*someone* I couldn't lose. And now these bastards thought they could take her away from me?

They were dead wrong.

The industrial area came into view—miles of rusted-out factories mixed with those still in use. The whole place looked forgotten, empty, and eerie as hell.

Shadow lifted his hand, signaling us to stop in front of one of the abandoned buildings. We killed the engines and split into two groups, leaving the bikes behind with the van. The last thing we wanted was to blow our cover with the sound of motorcycles.

"We'll check the abandoned ones first," Viking said, his voice low but firm.

The first two buildings came up empty, and my frustration simmered closer to boiling. My fists clenched at my sides, the weight of every passing minute threatening to crush me.

I *knew* what could happen to women taken like Shay. I'd seen it. We all had. That's why we were so careful—why Shadow had put a tracker in Mary's arm. I used to think it was overkill, but now? I'd tattoo one into Shay myself if it meant keeping her safe.

"Stop. Look over there," Lord whispered, pointing to a building up ahead.

My heart slammed against my ribs as I turned.

There it was—*the van*. Parked beside several motorcycles and a couple of beat-up cars.

"That's it," I growled, already moving. I didn't give a fuck about strategy—I just knew Shay was close, and I wasn't waiting another second.

Viking's iron grip closed around my arm, yanking me back. "Wait, Fuse. We need to call the others. We can't go in until everyone's here."

"They could be hurting her right now!" I hissed, my voice raw with rage.

"He's right, Fuse," Moreno added, stepping in front of me. "Going in half-cocked will get you and her killed. You want to save Shay? Then pull your shit together and wait for the others."

I sucked in a breath, my entire body vibrating with the need to act. They were right, but every fiber of me was ready to tear those fuckers apart with my bare hands.

"They better fucking hurry," I ground out, rolling my shoulders, trying to stop the rage from swallowing me whole. My eyes locked on that building ahead, my mind a storm of what-ifs.

I was so close to her. *So close.*

The others better get here fast because when we went in, I wasn't holding back. Not an inch.

And those bastards? They'd wish they'd never laid eyes on my little rockstar.

23

It wasn't long before more bikers showed up and all members of the Fire Dragons assholes. Their leather jackets were emblazoned with their symbol - a fiery dragon breathing flames. They exuded an aura of danger and recklessness, fueled by drugs and alcohol.

I watched in dread as they surrounded our group, Mark and Steve taking the brunt of their aggressive behavior. My heart raced with fear and helplessness, knowing that I was at the mercy of these ruthless men. The thought of being violated and raped made me want to scream, but I knew I had to stay quiet if I wanted to survive.

But my thoughts were interrupted by one of the bikers - nicknamed "Scab"—as he kneeled down in front of me, his greasy appearance making my skin crawl. With a cruel grin, he tore off my shirt and bra, exposing my breasts. He was so damn disgusting, he needed a shower and a breath mint.

"They said we couldn't touch you, but they didn't say we couldn't use you in other ways," Scab taunted. "Small tits, but they'll have to do. I'm gonna rub one out while you watch."

My body shuddered with disgust as the dirty asshole stroked himself, taunting me with his intentions. I turned my head away, refusing to look at him.

Before I could react or look away, another biker named "Mouth" joined in, holding my head in place so I couldn't escape Scab's lewd display. The situation felt like a nightmare, and I desperately wished it wasn't real.

Suddenly, there was a loud gunshot, causing chaos and confusion among the bikers. In a split second, Scab's head exploded as he fell to the ground, lifeless. Mouth released me in shock as I leaned back against the wall, trying to process what had just happened.

My ex-boyfriend Shawn walked into the room, gun still smoking in his hand. My mind struggled to make sense of this bizarre turn of events - why was he here? And how did he know these dangerous bikers?

But my questions were brushed aside as Shawn approached me, his eyes greedily scanning my naked body. Despite everything we had been through, there was no denying that he still found me attractive, his thumb caressing my nipples with possessiveness.

"You bastards were instructed not to touch her," a very familiar voice snarled. What the ever-loving fuck? I thought he had finally given up on bothering me. He leaned down and caressed my nipples. "Still as sexy as ever, Shay," he smirked.

"What the hell are you doing, Shawn?" I snapped at him, demanding answers. But before I could get any, he backhanded me across the face, causing pain and shock to course through me. This wasn't the man I thought I loved. No, this was a cruel and twisted version of him.

"Still have that attitude and you better learn to curb that shit," he growled. "It'll get you killed."

"What are you doing this?" I asked, trying to get answers. "You're the one who cheated on me!"

"Those whores didn't mean shit. I did it to spare you from some of my rougher forms of play, but now you can fucking take it all, the rough, the perverted, and whatever else I decide."

With each word he spoke, my disbelief grew - Shawn had been using other women to "spare" me from his rough and dirty sexual needs? And now, he wanted to unleash all that pent-up violence on me?

It was too much to comprehend, but I knew one thing for sure - I needed to find a way out of this situation before it got even more dangerous.

"I help the Fire Dragons with their business when they pass through Baltimore," he began, his voice dripping with malice. "And when I heard you had ties to the club they were after, I made a deal. They could use you to draw out The Devil's House, and I could keep you for myself."

I looked at him in disbelief. How could he have possibly known about my past involvement with the club? But then again, Shawn always seemed to know everything.

"What makes you think they'll come for me?" I tried to say calmly, though my heart was racing with fear.

"Don't play dumb with me, Shay," he shot back, getting closer to me. "I know you're fucking one of them. Your dad was one of them too; your mom is still there." He kneeled down in front of me, his eyes boring into mine. "No denial, Shay? Does he fuck better than me?" Without giving me a chance to respond, he continued his tirade. "You fucking betrayed me and now I have a punishment for you."

With unexpected force, he grabbed my right wrist and twisted it until I heard a sickening snap. My cry of pain caught my throat as I stared at him in shock.

"Now play that precious guitar of yours," he sneered.

As if on cue, one of the men spoke up. "This sentimental crap can wait. We need to move. Cross wants videos sent to Shadow at The Devil's House, letting him know we have their property."

My head reeled from the pain and confusion as they untied my wrists and forced me to stand up. Looking over at my unconscious friends who had been beaten bloody, I wondered if Fuse and the club would come to save us in time. But for now, we were at the mercy of Shawn and his twisted vendetta against me.

24

We were ready to go in. Vampire and Soldier, both snipers, were in the building across from this one. They could give us information based on what they saw through the window and have our backs if needed. So far, we knew there were at least eight guys on the inside, plus Shay and her band members.

Viking, Lord, and Moreno headed around the front of the building, while Shadow, Stonewall, and I headed to the back. There were two Fire Dragons guarding the back entrance. We took them by surprise, using silencers on our guns; we didn't want to alert the fuckers inside. Shadow killing one man, me the other, was almost too easy.

We made our way into the building. We knew about where they were. Once outside the room, they were being held in, the other brothers joining us. Vampire was communicating with Shadow through a headset. I saw concern cross Shadow's face, and I knew something was happening inside that room.

Shadow whispered, "Soldier and Vampire are ready. The men inside don't have their guns out, at least that they can see. So we should have the element of surprise. They are all on the left when we get to the door." He stopped and looked at me. "Fuse, don't let anything you see distract you. It could get you or Shay killed, understand?"

I knew then that I wouldn't like what I was going to find. I prepared myself to get ready for the kill.

Shadow gave the signal, and we shoved the door open, rushing into the room, guns drawn. I saw Shay in the corner, some bastard over her. I steeled myself to stay methodical. One by one, the men fell between our shots, and Vampire and Soldier picked them off to the sound of shattering glass. These men were sloppy. You can't be in this life and not train for this shit.

My focus went to Shay, an abused Shay.

Her face told me all I needed to know—seeing the man crouching beside her. I saw red and rage boiling inside me. I brought my leg around, kicking him in the head, then picking him up. I started beating the fucker who dared touch Shay. Blood was pouring from him as I hit him, shattering his face and then going to work on kicking the shit out of the rest of his body.

"Enough, Fuse, just kill the bastard so we can clean this shit up," Viking demanded, glowering at me.

The man was unconscious, so I didn't get the satisfaction of watching his face as I put a bullet in his head. Coming down from the rage, I looked around. Thank God they had taken Shay out of the room. I didn't want her to see me like that.

I needed to find Shay.

She was sitting in the open doors of the van, Soldier carefully wrapping her wrist. Her face was pinched in pain as she squinted, trying to tough it out.

The sight of her like that—hurt and vulnerable—hit me in the gut. I walked over, sat down beside her, and pulled her gently into my arms. I wasn't sure what those bastards had done to her, but I knew one thing: we hadn't gotten there a second too soon. She still had her pants on when we entered, which gave me some relief, but her shirt had been torn off. Someone had given her a replacement, and just thinking about what could've happened if we were an hour later made my blood boil.

"Shay's wrist is broken," Soldier said as he finished wrapping it. "Once we get back to the clubhouse, I'll call the doc to come take a look. She says there aren't any other injuries. Her bandmates are already headed to the clubhouse."

I looked down into Shay's eyes, searching for anything she wasn't telling me. "Are you sure? Nothing else?" My voice came out softer than I expected. I needed to *know*.

"No," she whispered, her voice steady despite everything. "I'm fine—more scared than anything. Did you... did you get the guy? The one who was in there when they dragged me out?"

How the hell was I supposed to answer that? I smirked, trying to ease her mind. "Let's just say he won't be bothering anyone again."

Her eyes softened for a moment, but then she looked away, guilt clouding her face. "It's my fault Mark and Steve got hurt."

"What?" I frowned, brushing a hand along her cheek, forcing her to look at me. "How in the hell is any of this your fault, Shay?"

She slumped forward, her shoulders heavy with a burden she didn't deserve to carry. "That man... the one in there was my ex, Shawn."

I froze, listening.

"He wanted me back," she said quietly, her voice laced with anger and regret. "He's a dirty cop. He was working with the Fire Dragons and cut some deal with them to get to me. I had no idea he'd gone this far—*no idea* he was such a crazy asshole." She swallowed hard. "He hurt Mark and Steve to punish me, just like breaking my wrist so I can't play. That's what he does—uses people against me."

"And Gabe?" I asked, trying to keep my voice calm.

"Gabe was Cross's cousin." She shook her head. "They threatened him, said they'd hurt his family if he didn't do what they wanted. He was the one sending me the letters, trying to warn me away. I guess... I guess he thought he was helping me by pushing me out of town."

Her words hit me like a punch to the gut. I couldn't blame her for being exhausted—she looked wrung out, physically and emotionally. Whatever had gone down in that room, I'd deal with it later. Right now, I just needed to get her out of here. She needed to see the doc, and Jane was worried sick back at the clubhouse. The cleanup was already starting, and Shay didn't need to see that shit.

"We'll talk more later, okay?" I said softly. "Right now, we need to get that wrist looked at. Do you think you can ride?"

She took a deep breath, squared her shoulders, and nodded with that same fire I'd come to expect from her. "Yeah, I can ride."

I couldn't stop the small smile tugging at my lips. *That's my girl.*

"Come on," I said, pulling her carefully to her feet. I wrapped an arm around her, holding her close as I led her to my bike. Once she was settled on the back, her arms gently wrapped around me, I kicked the engine to life.

As we tore down the road, the wind whipping past us, I felt her pressed against me—solid and real. I realized something right then.

I *always* wanted her here.

My little rockstar.

I didn't lie to Fuse—I was more scared than anything. The broken wrist? I could handle that. But the *other*... that would've broken me. Shawn wasn't the man I once knew; the brutal way he came at me today proved that. Just thinking about it made my stomach turn.

He was going to rape me while those sleazy bastards recorded it.

I'd never been so relieved to see anyone in my life as I was when Fuse and the others stormed that room. The way they took control was a blur of chaos and precision. Before I could even register what was happening, Viking carried me out, and the last thing I saw was Fuse kicking Shawn.

I wasn't a fool—I knew Shawn was dead.

The Devil's House wouldn't let him walk away after what he'd done.

On the surface, the club looked tame, but beneath that, it was still a one-percenter club through and through. Fuse had always been my sexy biker, the cocky charmer who made me melt, but today I saw a different side of him—a side I didn't know existed. As brutal as it was, I couldn't help but respect the way the club had handled everything, as if it was just another day on the job.

When we finally pulled into the clubhouse, relief washed over me, though exhaustion was hot on its heels. Riding with Fuse was one thing, but the ache in my wrist and the weight of everything that had happened started to hit me. I saw my mom waiting out front, her face etched with worry. She was already crying by the time I swung my leg off the bike.

She rushed to me, pulling me into her arms. "Shay! Are you okay? Oh my baby..." Her tears triggered mine, and suddenly we were both crying like fools.

"Come on, Jane, let her go. Shay needs to get looked at," Silver said gently, nudging her out of the way.

"Okay, baby girl, what hurts? I'm coming with you," Mom said, brushing tears from her face.

"Is Doc here?" Fuse asked, his voice firm but calm.

"Yeah, he's in the medical room with the other two," Silver replied.

"Come on, I'll walk you back," Fuse said, taking my arm while Mom flanked my other side.

I had no idea there was a medical room in the clubhouse. Shadow had seriously upped the game—modernized the place in ways I couldn't imagine. He wasn't anything like his father. We walked to the very back of the clubhouse, Fuse opening a door I hadn't even noticed before.

The room stunned me. It looked just like a small emergency room—four hospital beds, medical equipment, and everything. Two beds were already occupied by Mark and Steve, a man in his thirties tending to them.

"Shay, this is Doc Kenny. He'll fix you right up," Fuse said, guiding me toward one of the empty beds.

"*Doc* Kenny?" I asked, raising an eyebrow. This guy didn't look like any doctor I'd ever seen. With his jet-black hair, piercing green eyes, and a body that looked like it belonged on a fitness magazine, he was far from your typical doctor. He wore tight jeans, a fitted t-shirt, and black biker boots. A *doctor*? Really?

Fuse smirked, knowing exactly what I was thinking. "Trust me, he knows what he's doing. I have to go talk to Shadow. I'll be back before you're done." He gave me a quick kiss on the head and left.

I looked over at Mom, who was now quietly talking to Mark and Steve. Guilt gnawed at me as I saw them both battered and bruised. "How are you guys holding up?" I asked, my voice softer than I intended.

Mark grinned, despite the cut on his lip. "We look worse than we are, Shay. We'll heal. Things could've been a hell of a lot worse."

"How about you?" Steve asked, his tone full of concern.

I forced a small smile. "Broken wrist. Shawn decided I didn't need to play guitar for a while." I ran my fingers through my hair, trying to sound unfazed, even though his actions still twisted in my gut. Playing had always been my therapy, my escape—and Shawn tried to take that from me.

"*Shawn?*" Mom, Mark, and Steve said at the same time, their faces a mix of shock and anger.

"Yeah," I sighed. "I'll fill you in after I'm fixed up."

Doc Kenny stood patiently to the side, clearly waiting for me to finish. "Whenever you're ready, Shay. We need to x-ray that wrist," he said, motioning to the small room at the back.

I slid off the bed, following him, but I couldn't help but stifle a giggle. What kind of doctor wore biker boots?

Doc's green eyes flicked toward me, a smirk on his lips.

"Something funny, Shay?"

I smiled innocently. "You just don't look like any doctor I've ever seen."

"Well," he said, winking, "looks can be deceiving. Trust me—I know what I'm doing. Now let's get that wrist checked."

An hour later, my wrist was set in a cast, and I was stuck with the damn thing for six to eight weeks. Doc Kenny was good—quick, efficient, and professional, despite his unconventional look. As frustrating as it was to be sidelined, I knew I was lucky. It could've been so much worse.

And honestly? Right now, a broken wrist felt like a blessing.

25

Leaving Shay with Doc gave me a moment to breathe. Doc used to practice medicine but left it behind when he went nomad years ago. He's been thinking about becoming a full-time member again, and Shadow's newly finished medical room couldn't have come at a better time. Some situations can't be handled in a hospital—too much attention, too many questions—and this was definitely one of those times.

I caught Shadow just as he was coming through the door, looking as calm as ever. "Hey, Shadow. Everything get cleaned up okay?" I asked.

"Yeah," Shadow replied with a nod. "The whole operation took under two hours. Lucky for us, there weren't any occupied buildings nearby. We did manage to take one man alive, though—he's being handled in the basement as we speak. How's Shay and her friends?"

"The guys look beat up but nothing serious. Shay's got a broken wrist but no other injuries. She mentioned something about the Fire Dragons—info we'll want to know. I'll question her and bring it to church," I said, keeping my tone steady. Truth was, I wanted to be the one to talk to Shay. No way was I letting anyone else put her through that.

"That'll work. Viking's going to talk to her friends. They need to forget what they saw—for their safety and ours. I'm holding off on calling church until tomorrow. I want all the pieces of this puzzle in place first." Shadow glanced toward the stairs, clearly eager to get to Mary.

"Got it. I just wanted to check in, but I'm heading back to Shay now." I turned and walked away, my mind already on her.

When I found Shay, she was sitting on the bed surrounded by her mom and friends, looking pale and exhausted. She was talking quietly, trying to stay strong for their sake. But I could see the weight of everything catching up to her.

I walked over, crouching next to her. "Come on, Shay. You need to rest, and I'm sure your friends are ready to get some sleep too."

She didn't argue. That was how I knew she was spent—my little rockstar usually had a comeback for everything. She hugged her mom and friends before slipping her hand into mine. I led her out and up to her room, keeping her close.

Once we were alone, I took care of her. I stripped her down gently, helped her into the shower, and stayed close, steadying her as the warm water washed away the day's grime. She leaned into me, letting me take care of her, no walls between us for once.

When I got her into bed, I pulled her close, wrapping myself around her. "Get some sleep, little rockstar. You need it," I whispered, pressing a kiss to her temple.

Her breathing slowed almost immediately as she fell into sleep, the kind of deep, heavy sleep that comes after too much fear and exhaustion. I tightened my hold, unwilling to let her slip away—not tonight, not ever.

With her pressed against me, safe in my arms, I finally let myself relax. I wasn't far behind her, drifting into sleep with the faint scent of her shampoo and the sound of her steady breathing grounding me.

She was here. That was all that mattered.

Waking up next to Fuse, I could feel his gaze on me before I even opened my eyes. When I finally looked up at him, his face was serious, his amber eyes watching me with an intensity that made my heart flutter.

"You look thoughtful this morning," I said softly, my voice still heavy with sleep.

"I love you, Shay," Fuse blurted out, his hand coming up to stroke my face gently.

My breath hitched. Of all the things I thought he might say, *that* was the last. "What?" I whispered, blinking at him in disbelief.

"Fuck," he muttered, rubbing his jaw. "I didn't mean to just throw it out there like that. But it's the truth, Shay. I don't know how or when it happened, but from the first moment I saw you, there was this feeling... like you belonged to me. Like you were mine. I can't explain it, but it's like I've known you forever, and now—hell—I can't picture my life without you in it." He paused, his voice growing quieter. "At the same time, I'm scared shitless because no woman has ever stuck around for me. I always screw things up."

I stared at him for a moment, searching his face. The vulnerability there cracked something open inside me. "Fuse, you're not a screw-up," I said firmly. "You just haven't had the right woman yet. I'm scared too, you know. But I love you." The words slipped out, surprising even me. "And that scares the shit out of me, but..." I hesitated, a small smile tugging at my lips, "you have this pull on me that I can't fight. I decided I'm not going to fight it anymore. I'm just going to let it happen."

"Are you sure you want to take a chance on me, Shay?" His voice was low, rough, but there was hope in it, just beneath the surface. "I can be a dumbass sometimes. And the club... are you okay with all of this? With what comes with me?"

I cupped his face, brushing my thumb along his jawline. "Don't you worry, Fuse. I'll hold you accountable for all the dumb shit you do —*as long as that dumb shit doesn't include another woman.*" My eyes narrowed slightly to drive my point home. "If it ever does, my earlier threat stands. I'm out, no discussion."

He smirked, that cocky grin of his softening as he took in my words. "Fair enough."

"And as for the club," I continued, meeting his gaze, "I can live with it. It's a part of who you are. But you'll have to live with me and my band traveling at times." A flicker of doubt crossed my mind as I said it. *If I still have a band.* Gabe's betrayal had shaken us all, and I wasn't sure where we stood.

Fuse frowned slightly, picking up on my hesitation. "You're not losing the band, Shay. I know it's been a rough week, but you'll figure it out. You're too damn talented not to."

The confidence in his voice made my chest tighten. I didn't know how this man—this rough-around-the-edges biker—could make me feel so understood, so seen. "I hope you're right," I said quietly.

Fuse leaned down, pressing a kiss to my forehead. "I'm always right, little rockstar."

I laughed softly, rolling my eyes at him. "Cocky bastard."

He grinned against my skin. "Only for you."

In that moment, everything felt right—raw and uncertain, but right. For the first time in a long time, I wasn't fighting to protect myself. I wasn't holding back. I was letting love in, risks and all.

"I'll take that deal, Shay. Now my cock wants to seal the deal. How is the arm? Are you up to it?" I could feel his erection poking me as his hands started roaming.

"You bet I'm up to it; I'll try not to clock you with this cast, but no guarantees," I chuckled as his caresses turned demanding.

He pinned me down, using his muscular arms to hold himself above me. His fingers traced my features with gentle precision as he kissed every inch of my face, lingering on each eyelid before moving to my cheek and lips. He teased and tortured me with his mouth, teasing my lips before plunging his hot tongue deep inside. My body pulsed with desire as he matched the rhythm of his tongue with his hips.

As Fuse's lips made their way to my chest, his hot breath and skilled tongue sent sparks flying through my body. I arched my back, offering myself completely to him. But he didn't stop there; no, he continued his descent until his mouth was grazing over my most sensitive area. With expert fingers and a wicked tongue, Fuse drove me wild until I thought I couldn't take it anymore.

Just when I was about to reach the peak of pleasure, he pulled away. I looked at him in frustration but quickly melted into bliss as he entered me with force. My body instantly responded, lighting up with electricity as we moved together in perfect harmony. Before I knew it, another wave of intense pleasure washed over me, causing me to scream out in ecstasy.

We collapsed beside each other, both panting and glowing with satisfaction. "I can never get enough of you," Fuse breathed into my ear as he pulled me close.

"Same here," I replied between heavy breaths. "But if we're going to keep doing this, let's make sure we have some birth control on hand next time."

"Shit, Shay, I'm sorry." Fuse's expression turned serious as he realized what had happened in the heat of the moment. "I'll make sure to have condoms ready next time."

"It's not only your responsibility," I reminded him, feeling a rush of guilt for not speaking up sooner.

"I need to shower and get to the garage. What about you?" Fuse changed the subject, giving me a playful slap on the ass as he got up. "I have a feeling you're going to need some rest after that."

"Yeah, I think so too." I couldn't help but feel a tinge of sadness in my voice as I remembered everything that had happened recently.

"Just relax and stay at the clubhouse today. Maybe check on Mark and Steve too," Fuse suggested, his expression softening with concern.

"I will." I nodded, grateful for his understanding.

As we headed towards the shower, my mind was already racing with anticipation. This time, I would make sure that Fuse wouldn't be the only one driving me wild. With a mischievous grin, I followed him into the bathroom, ready to take control and give him a taste of his own medicine.

26

It's been about two months since everything went down with Shawn. Fuse and I have been exploring our feelings for each other, and what we've found is solid—*unshakable*. Our love has only grown stronger, and now I wear Fuse's property patch proudly.

The cast is finally off, courtesy of the ever-sexy Dr. Kenny, who assured me my wrist has healed well and there'll be no lasting issues. I can play my guitar again, which feels like a blessing. Mark, Steve, and I sat down and decided to keep the band going. We agreed to let what happened stay in the past. The music is too important to us to just let it go. Mark and Steve even decided to stick around, taking Shadow's advice to stay local—it's safer that way.

"Watch your head," Fuse said as he carried me into our room at a cheesy Las Vegas hotel.

And why are we in Las Vegas? Well, it turns out Fuse has some *strong swimmers*, and I'm now six weeks pregnant. Since Shadow and Mary's wedding is next month—and Shadow promised Mary's dad that she'd get the wedding of her dreams—Fuse and I decided we didn't want to steal their spotlight. So here we are, married by an Elvis impersonator in a chapel that fits us perfectly—funny, impulsive, and a little wild.

The only people who know we're married and expecting are my mom, Silver, and Shadow. Shadow had to okay the two weeks we took to ride out here on Fuse's bike. Honestly, I loved every minute of that ride. It gave Fuse and me some much-needed alone time before the chaos of a new baby. We both know that kind of quiet won't come easy once the baby arrives.

We've decided to live at the clubhouse for a while, at least until we get our footing. Mom will be there to help, which is a relief because, truth be told, neither Fuse nor I have any idea what we're doing when it comes to babies.

Fuse set me carefully on the bed, crouching to kiss my stomach, his lips lingering against the small bump. "We did it, little rockstar. You and me—this is it. For life."

I smiled, my heart full. "Yep. It's me or death, Loverboy. Remember that." I winked at him, teasing.

He grinned, flopping down beside me on the bed with a laugh. "It would take death to get me away from you, and even then, I'd come back and haunt your ass, Shay."

"Fuse," I said softly, reaching for him, "shut up and get over here." My voice dropped to a whisper, "Play with me."

His smile turned wicked as he leaned in. "You don't have to ask me twice, little rockstar."

And play with me he did—*all night long.*

The End

* * *

Player
Leather
MHAIRI O'REILLY
West Virginia
Jones
Valley
MHAIRI O'REILLY

Coming Soon
SPINNER'S
BELLA
Mhairi O'Reilly

New South Carolina Series Book One Available Now.

* * *

"Beneath the hottest flames lies the woman I was meant to have. Only, she's determined to burn me to ashes."

BOLT'S
flame

THE DEVIL'S HOUSE
South Carolina
BOOK ONE

A NOVEL BY MHAIRI O'REILLY

***

Mhairi O'Reilly lives in Upstate, South Carolina. A native of West Virginia, Mhairi loves to read. Devoting many hours of her life to it. She always dreamed of writing her own stories, when the time arrived that she had the time, she jumped into it, not looking back.

Made in the USA
Columbia, SC
04 March 2025